HOW TO KILL A MONSTER

Look for other **Goosebumps** books
by R.L. Stine:

The Abominable Snowman of Pasadena
The Barking Ghost
The Cuckoo Clock of Doom
The Curse of the Mummy's Tomb
Deep Trouble
Egg Monsters From Mars
Ghost Beach
Ghost Camp
The Ghost Next Door
The Haunted Mask
The Horror at Camp Jellyjam
How I Got My Shrunken Head
It Came From Beneath the Sink!
Let's Get Invisible!
Monster Blood
Night of the Living Dummy
One Day at HorrorLand
Say Cheese and Die!
The Scarecrow Walks at Midnight
A Shocker on Shock Street
Stay Out of the Basement
Welcome to Camp Nightmare
Welcome to Dead House
The Werewolf of Fever Swamp

Goosebumps®

HOW TO KILL A MONSTER

R.L. STINE

SCHOLASTIC INC.
New York Toronto London Auckland Sydney
Mexico City New Delhi Hong Kong Buenos Aires

The *Goosebumps* book series created by Parachute Press, Inc.

ISBN 0-439-56836-6

12 11 10 9 8 7 6 5 4   5 6 7 8/0

Printed in the U.S.A.   40

First Scholastic printing, August 1996

1

"Why do we have to go there?" I wailed from the backseat of the car. "Why?"

"Gretchen, I've told you three times *why*." Dad sighed. "Your mother and I have to go to Atlanta. For work!"

"I know that," I replied, leaning over the front seat. "But why can't we go with you? Why do we have to stay with Grandma and Grandpa?"

"Because we said so," Mom and Dad declared together.

Because we said so. Once they said those deadly words, there was no use arguing.

I slumped down in my seat.

Mom and Dad had some kind of work emergency in Atlanta. They got the call this morning.

It's not fair, I thought. They get to visit a cool city like Atlanta. And Clark — my stepbrother — and I have to go to Mud Town.

Mud Town.

Well, it's not really called Mud Town. But it

1

should be. Because it's a swamp. Grandma Rose and Grandpa Eddie live in southern Georgia — in a swamp.

Can you believe it?

A swamp.

I stared out the car window. We'd been riding on highways all day. Now we were driving on a narrow road through the swamp.

It was late afternoon. And the cypress trees began to cast long shadows over the marshy grass.

I stuck my head out the window. A blast of hot, humid air hit my face. I ducked back in and turned to Clark. His nose was buried in a comic book.

Clark is twelve — like me. He's much shorter than I am. Much shorter. And he has curly brown hair, brown eyes, and tons of freckles. He looks exactly like Mom.

I'm kind of tall for my age. I have long, straight blond hair and green eyes. I look like Dad.

My parents divorced when I turned two years old. The same thing happened to Clark. My dad and his mom married each other right after our third birthdays, and we all moved into a new house together.

I like my stepmother. And Clark and I get along okay, I guess. He acts like a jerk sometimes. Even my friends say so. But I think their brothers act like jerks, too.

I stared at Clark.

Watched him read.

2

His glasses slid down his nose.

He pushed them up.

"Clark . . ." I started.

"Shhhh." He waved his hand at me. "I'm at the good part."

Clark loves comic books. Scary ones. But he's not brave — so he's always terrified by the time he finishes.

I glanced out the window again.

I stared at the trees. At the branches, all draped in long gray webs. They dangled from every tree — curtains of gray. They made the swamp look really gloomy.

Mom told me about the gray webs when we were packing this morning. She knows a lot about swamps. She thinks swamps are pretty — in a spooky sort of way.

Mom said the gray webs were actually a swamp plant that grew right on the trees.

A plant that grows on a plant. Weird, I thought. Definitely weird.

Almost as weird as Grandma and Grandpa.

"Dad, how come Grandma and Grandpa never visit us?" I asked. "We haven't seen them since we were four."

"Well, they're a little strange." Dad peered at me through the rearview mirror. "They don't like to travel. They almost never leave their house. And they live so far back in the swamp, it's very hard to visit them."

"Oh, wow!" I said. "A sleepover with two strange old hermits."

"Smelly, strange old hermits," Clark mumbled, glancing up from his comic.

"Clark! Gretchen!" Mom scolded. "Don't talk about your grandparents that way."

"They're not my grandparents. They're hers." Clark jerked his head toward me. "And they do smell. I can still remember it."

I punched my stepbrother in the arm. But he was right. Grandma and Grandpa did smell. Like a combination of mildew and mothballs.

I sank deep into my seat and let out a loud yawn.

It seemed as if we'd been riding in the car for weeks. And it was really crowded back there — with me, Clark, and Charley kind of squished together. Charley is our dog — a golden retriever.

I pushed Charley out of the way and stretched out.

"Quit shoving him onto me!" Clark complained. His comic book dropped to the floor.

"Sit still, Gretchen," Mom muttered. "I knew we should have boarded Charley."

"I tried to find a kennel for him," Dad said. "But no one could take him at the last minute."

Clark pushed Charley off his lap and reached down for his comic. But I grabbed it first.

"Oh, brother," I moaned when I read the title. "*Creatures from the Muck*? How can you read this garbage?"

4

"It's not garbage," Clark shot back. "It's really cool. Better than those stupid nature magazines you read."

"What's it about?" I asked, flipping through the pages.

"It's about some totally gross monsters. Half-human. Half-beast. They set traps to catch people. Then they hide under the mud. Near the surface," Clark explained. He grabbed the comic from my hand.

"Then what happens?" I asked.

"They wait. They wait as long as it takes — for the humans to fall in their traps." Clark's voice started to quiver. "Then they force them deep into the swamp. And make them their slaves!"

Clark shuddered. He glanced out the window. Out at the eerie cypress trees with their long beards of gray.

It was growing dark now. The trees' shadows shifted over the tall grass.

Clark lowered himself in his seat. He has a wild imagination. He really believes the stuff he reads. Then he gets scared — like now.

"Do they do anything else?" I asked. I wanted Clark to tell me more. He was really scaring himself good.

"Well, at night, the monsters rise up from the mud," he went on, sliding down in his seat some more. "And they drag kids from their beds. They drag them into the swamp. They drag them down into the mud. No one ever sees the kids again. Ever."

Clark was totally freaked now.

"There really are creatures like that in the swamp. I read about them in school," I lied. "Horrible monsters. Half-alligator, half-human. Covered with mud. With spiky scales underneath, hidden. If you just brush against one, the scales rip the flesh right off your bones."

"Gretchen, stop," Mom warned.

Clark hugged Charley close to him.

"Hey! Clark!" I pointed out the window to an old narrow bridge up ahead. Its wooden planks sagged. It looked ready to crumble. "I bet a swamp monster is waiting for us under that bridge."

Clark gazed out the window at the bridge. He hugged Charley closer to him.

Dad began steering the car over the old wooden planks. They rumbled and groaned under the weight.

I held my breath as we slowly rolled across. This bridge can't hold us, I thought. No way.

Dad drove very, very slowly.

It seemed to take forever to ride across.

Clark clung to Charley. He kept his eyes out the window, glued to the bridge.

When we finally neared the end, I let out a long whoosh of air.

And then I gasped — as a deafening explosion rocked the car.

"Nooo!" Clark and I both screamed as the car swerved wildly.

Skidded out of control.

It crashed into the side of the old bridge.

Plowed right through the old wood.

"We—we're going down!" Dad cried.

I shut my eyes as we plunged into the swamp.

2

We hit hard, with a loud *thud*.

Clark and Charley bounced all over the backseat. When the car finally slid to a stop, they were sitting on top of me.

"Is everyone okay?" Mom asked in a shaky voice. She turned to the back.

"Uh-huh," I replied. "I guess."

We all sat quietly for a moment.

Charley broke the silence with a soft whimper.

"Wh-what happened?" Clark stammered.

"Flat tire." Dad sighed. "I hope the spare is okay. There's no way we're going to get help at night in the middle of a swamp."

I leaned out the window to check out the tire. Dad was right. It was totally flat.

Boy, were we lucky, I thought. Lucky this was a low bridge. Otherwise . . .

"Okay, everybody out of the car," Mom interrupted my thoughts. "So Dad can change the tire."

Clark took a long look out the car window before he opened the door. I could tell he was afraid.

"Better be careful, Clark," I said as he swung his short, stubby legs out the door. "The swamp monster likes low targets."

"That's funny, Gretchen. Really funny. Remind me to laugh."

Dad headed for the trunk to find the jack. Mom followed. Clark and I stepped into the swamp.

"Oh, gross!" My brand-new white high-tops sank into the thick black mud.

I let out a long sigh.

How could anyone live in a swamp? I wanted to know. It was so gross out here.

The air felt thick and soupy. So hot, it was hard to breathe.

As I pulled my hair back into a scrunchie, I glanced around.

I couldn't see much. The sky had darkened to black.

Clark and I drifted away from the car. "Let's explore while Dad fixes the tire," I suggested.

"I don't think that's such a great idea," Clark murmured.

"Sure it is," I urged. "There's nothing else to do. And it's better than standing around here, waiting. Isn't it?"

"I — I guess," Clark stammered.

We took a few steps into the swamp. My face began to tingle and itch.

Mosquitoes! Hundreds of them.

We ducked and dodged, frantically brushing them off our faces, off our bare arms.

"Yuck! It's disgusting out here!" Clark cried. "I'm not staying here. I'm going to Atlanta!"

"It's not this buggy at Grandma's house," Mom called out.

"Oh, sure." Clark rolled his eyes. "I'm going back to the car."

"Come on," I insisted. "Let's just see what's over there." I pointed to a patch of tall grass up ahead.

I stomped through the mud, glancing over my shoulder — to make sure Clark was following me. He was.

As we reached the grass, we could hear a loud rustling deep in the blades. Clark and I peered down, straining to see in the dark.

"Don't wander too far," Dad warned, as he and Mom pulled our luggage from the trunk, searching for a flashlight. "There might be snakes out there."

"Snakes? Whoa!" Clark jumped away. He started running full speed back to the car.

"Don't be a baby!" I called after him. "Let's do some exploring."

"No way!" He choked out the words. "And don't call me a baby."

"I'm sorry," I apologized. "Come on. We'll walk over to that tree. The one that towers over the others. It's not that far away. Then we'll come right back," I promised. "Puh-lease."

Clark and I started toward the tree.

We walked slowly. Through the darkness. Through the jungle of cypress trees.

The curtains of gray swayed on the tree branches. They were so thick — thick enough to hide behind.

It would be real easy to get lost in here, I realized. Lost forever.

I shuddered as the heavy gray curtains brushed against my skin. They felt like spiderwebs. Huge, sticky spiderwebs.

"Come on, Gretchen. Let's turn back," Clark pleaded. "It's gross out here."

"Just a little further," I urged him on.

We made our way carefully through the trees, sloshing through puddles of inky water.

Tiny bugs buzzed in my ears. Bigger ones bit at my neck. I swatted them away.

I stepped forward — onto a dry, grassy patch of ground. "Whoa!"

The patch started to move. Started to float across the black water.

I leaped off — and stumbled on a tree root. No — not a tree root. "Hey, Clark. Look at this!" I bent to get a better look.

"What is *that*?" Clark kneeled beside me and peered at the knobby form.

"It's called a cypress knee," I explained. "Mom

11

told me about them. They grow near the cypress trees. They rise up from the roots."

"How come Mom never tells *me* about these things?" he demanded.

"I guess she doesn't want to scare you," I replied.

"Yeah, right," he muttered, pushing up his glasses. "Want to go back now?"

"We're almost there. See?" I said, pointing to the tall tree. It stood in a small clearing just a few feet away.

Clark followed me into the clearing.

The air smelled sour here.

The night sounds of the swamp echoed in the darkness. We could hear low moans. Shrill cries. The moans and cries of swamp creatures, I thought. Hidden swamp creatures.

A shiver ran down my spine.

I moved deeper into the clearing. The tree with the high branches stood right before me.

Clark stumbled over a log. Stumbled into a black pool of mucky water.

"That's it," he groaned. "I'm outta here."

Even in the dark, I could see the frightened expression on Clark's face.

It *was* scary in the swamp. But Clark seemed so petrified that I started to giggle.

And then I heard the footsteps.

Clark heard them too.

Heavy, thudding footsteps across the black, misty swamp.

Charging closer.

Headed straight for us.

"Come on!" Clark cried, yanking on my arm. "Time to go!"

But I didn't move. I *couldn't* move.

Now I could hear the creature's breathing. Heavy, rasping breaths. Nearer. Nearer.

It came springing out. From behind the gray-bearded tree limbs.

A tall black form. A huge swamp creature. Loping toward us. Darker than the black swamp mud — with glowing red eyes.

3

"Charley — ! What are you doing down there?" Mom cried, marching into the clearing. "I thought you kids were watching him."

Charley?

I'd forgotten all about Charley.

Charley was the swamp monster.

"I've been looking all over for you," Mom snapped angrily. "Didn't we tell you to stay by the car? Dad and I have been searching everywhere."

"Sorry, Mom," I apologized. I couldn't say any more. Charley leaped on me and knocked me down — into the mud.

"Off! Charley! Off!" I shouted. But he planted his huge paws on my shoulders and licked my face.

I was covered in mud. Totally covered.

"Come on, boy." Clark tugged on Charley's collar. "You were scared, Gretchen. You thought Charley was a swamp monster." Clark laughed. "You were really scared."

"I — I was not," I sputtered, wiping the mud from my jeans. "I was just trying to scare you."

"You were really scared. Just admit it," Clark insisted. "Just admit it."

"I was NOT scared." My voice started to rise. "Who was the one begging to go back?" I reminded him. "You! You! You!"

"What's all the fighting about?" Dad demanded. "And what are you two doing way out here? Didn't I tell you to stay near the car?"

"Um, sorry, Dad," I apologized. "But we were kind of bored, just waiting around."

"We! What do you mean *we*? It was all Gretchen's idea," Clark protested. "She was the one who wanted to explore the swamp."

"That's enough!" Dad scolded. "Everyone — back to the car."

Clark and I argued all the way back. Charley trotted by my side, flinging more mud on my jeans.

The flat was fixed — but now Dad had to get the car back on the road. And it wasn't easy. Every time he stepped on the gas, the tires just spun around and around in the thick mud.

Finally, we all got out and pushed.

Now Mom and Clark were splattered with mud, too.

As we drove away, I stared out at the dark, eerie marsh.

And listened to the night sounds.

15

Sharp chitters.

Low moans.

Shrill cries.

I'd heard lots of stories about swamp monsters. And I'd read some ancient legends about them. Could they be real? I wondered. Do swamp monsters really exist?

Little did I know that I would soon find out the answer to that question. The hard way.

4

"Yes. Yes. They do."

"No way!" I told Dad. "That can't be where they live!"

"That's their house," Dad insisted as the car bumped up a narrow sandy road. "That's Grandma and Grandpa's house."

"That *can't* be their house." Clark rubbed his eyes. "It's a swamp mirage. I read about them in *Creatures from the Muck*. The swamp mud plays tricks on your eyes. It makes you see things."

See what I mean about Clark? He really does believe the stuff he reads.

And it was beginning to sound right to me, too. How else could you explain Grandma and Grandpa's house?

A castle.

A castle in the middle of a swamp.

Almost hidden in a grove of dark, towering trees.

Dad pulled the car up to the front door. I stared at the house in the glow of the headlights.

Three stories high. Built of dark gray stone. A turret rose up on the right side. On the left, a sliver of white smoke curled from a blackened chimney.

"I thought swamp houses were smaller," I murmured, "and built on stilts."

"That's the way they look in my comic," Clark agreed. "And what's with the windows?" His voice shook. "Are they vampires or something?"

I stared at the windows. They were tiny. And I could see only three of them. Three tiny windows in the entire house. One on each floor.

"Come on, kids," Mom said. "Let's get your luggage."

Mom, Dad, and Clark climbed out of the car and headed for the trunk. I stood by the car door with Charley.

The night air felt cold and damp on my skin.

I stared up.

Up at the big dark house. Almost hidden behind the trees. In the middle of nowhere.

And then I heard the howl. A mournful howl. From somewhere deep in the swamp.

A chill swept through me.

Charley pressed against my leg. I bent to pet him. "What could that be?" I whispered to the dog in the dark. "What kind of creature howls like that?"

"Gretchen. Gretchen." Mom waved from the front door of the house. Everyone else had gone inside.

"Oh, my," Grandma said as I stepped into the dim entrance. "This can't be our little Gretchen." She wrapped her frail arms around me and gave me a big hug.

She smelled just the way I had remembered — musty. I glanced at Clark. He rolled his eyes.

I stepped back and forced a smile.

"Move aside, Rose," Grandpa yelled. "Let me get a look at her."

"He's a little hard-of-hearing," Dad whispered to me.

Grandpa clasped my hand between his wrinkled fingers. He and Grandma seemed so slight. So fragile.

"We're really happy you're here!" Grandma exclaimed. Her blue eyes twinkled. "We don't get many visitors!"

"For a while, we thought you weren't coming!" Grandpa shouted. "We expected you hours ago."

"Flat tire," Dad explained.

"Tired?" Grandpa wrapped his arms around Dad. "Well, then come in and sit down, son."

Clark giggled. Mom shoved an elbow into his side. Grandpa and Grandma led us into the living room.

The room was enormous. Our whole house could probably fit inside it.

The walls were painted green. Drab green. I stared up at the ceiling. Up at an iron chandelier that held twelve candles, in a circle.

An enormous fireplace took up most of one wall.

The other walls were covered with black-and-white photographs. Yellowed with age.

Photographs everywhere. Of people I didn't recognize. Probably dead relatives, I thought.

I glanced through a doorway into the next room. The dining room. It appeared to be as big as the living room. Just as dark. Just as dreary.

Clark and I sat down on a tattered green couch. I felt the old springs sag under my weight. Charley groaned and stretched out on the floor at our feet.

I glanced around the room. At the pictures. At the worn rug. At the shabby tables and chairs. The flickering light high above us made our shadows dance on the dark walls.

"This place is creepy," Clark whispered. "And it really smells bad — worse than Grandma and Grandpa."

I choked back a laugh. But Clark was right. The room smelled strange. Damp and sour.

Why do two old people want to live like this? I wondered. In this musty, dark house. Deep in the swamp.

"Would anyone like something to drink?" Grandma interrupted my thoughts. "How about a nice cup of tea?"

Clark and I shook our heads no.

Mom and Dad also said no. They sat opposite us. The stuffing in their chairs spilled out the backs.

"Well, you're finally here!" Grandpa yelled to us. "It's just great. So, tell me — how come you were late?"

"Grandpa," Grandma shouted to him, "no more questions!" Then she turned to us. "After such a long trip, you must be starving. Come into the kitchen. I made my special chicken pot pie — just for you."

We followed Grandma and Grandpa into the kitchen. It looked like all the other rooms. Dark and dingy.

But it didn't smell as ancient as the other rooms. The tangy aroma of chicken pot pie floated through the air.

Grandma removed eight small pies from the oven. One for each of us — and a couple of extras in case we were starving, I guessed.

Grandma placed one on my plate, and I began to dig right in. I *was* starving.

As I lifted the fork to my mouth, Charley sprang up from his place on the floor and started to sniff.

He sniffed our chairs.

The counter.

The floor.

He leaped up to the table and sniffed.

"Charley, stop!" Dad ordered. "Down!"

Charley jumped from the table. Then he reared up in front of us — and curled his upper lip.

He let out a growl.

A low, menacing growl that erupted into loud barking.

Furious barking.

"What on earth is wrong with him?" Grandma demanded, frowning at the dog.

"I don't know," Dad told her. "He's never done that before."

"What is it, Charley?" I asked. I shoved my chair from the table and approached him.

Charley sniffed the air.

He barked.

He sniffed some more.

A chill of fear washed over me.

"What is it, boy? What do you smell?"

5

I grabbed Charley's collar. Petted him. Tried to calm him down. But he jerked out of my grasp.

He barked even louder.

I reached for his collar again and tugged him toward me. His nails scraped the floor as he pulled away.

The more I tugged on his collar, the harder Charley fought. He swung his head sharply from side to side. And started to growl.

"Easy, boy," I said softly. "Eeea — sy."

Nothing worked.

Finally Clark helped me drag Charley into the living room — where he started to settle down.

"What do you think is wrong with him?" Clark asked as we stroked the dog's head.

"I don't know." I stared down at Charley. Restless now, he turned in circles. Then he sat. Then turned in circles. Again and again.

"I just don't get it. He's never done that before. Ever."

Clark and I decided to wait in the living room with Charley while Mom and Dad finished eating. We weren't hungry anymore.

"How's that dog of yours?" Grandpa came in and sat down next to us. He ran his wrinkled fingers through his thinning gray hair.

"Better," Clark answered, pushing his glasses up.

"Pet her?" Grandpa hollered. "Sure! If you think that will help."

After dinner, Mom, Dad, Grandma, and Grandpa talked and talked — about practically everything that had happened since they last saw each other. Eight years ago.

Clark and I were bored. Really bored.

"Can we, um, watch television?" Clark finally asked.

"Oh, sorry, dear," Grandma apologized. "We don't have a television."

Clark glowered at me — as if it was my fault.

"Why don't you call Arnold?" I suggested. Arnold is the biggest nerd in our neighborhood. And Clark's best friend. "Remind him to pick up your new comic."

"Okay," Clark grumbled. "Um, where's the phone?"

"In town." Grandma smiled weakly. "We don't know many people — still alive. Doesn't pay to have a phone. Mr. Donner — at the general store — he takes messages for us."

"Haven't seen Donner all week, though," Grandpa added. "Our car broke down. Should be fixed soon. Any day now."

No television.

No phone.

No car.

In the middle of a swamp.

This time it was my turn to glower — at Mom and Dad.

I put on my angriest face. I was sure they were going to take us to Atlanta with them now. Absolutely sure.

Dad glanced at Mom. He opened his mouth to speak. Then he turned toward me. And shrugged an apology.

"Guess it's time for bed!" Grandpa checked his watch. "You two have to get an early start," he said to Mom and Dad.

"Tomorrow you're going to have so much fun," Grandma assured Clark and me.

"Yes, indeed," Grandpa agreed. "This big old house is great to explore. You'll have a real adventure!"

"And I'm going to bake my famous rhubarb pie!" Grandma exclaimed. "You kids can help me. You'll love it. It's so sweet, your teeth will fall out after one bite!"

I heard Clark gulp.

I groaned — loudly.

Mom and Dad ignored us. They said good night. And good-bye. They were leaving real early in the morning. Probably before we got up.

We followed Grandma up the dark, creaky old steps and down a long, winding hall to our rooms on the second floor.

Clark's room was right next to mine. I didn't have a chance to see what it looked like. After Clark went in, Grandma quickly ushered me to my room.

My room. My gloomy room.

I set my suitcase down next to the bed and glanced around. The room was nearly as big as a gym! And it didn't have a single window.

The only light came from a dim yellow bulb in a small lamp next to the bed.

A handmade rug covered the floor. Worn thin in spots, its rings of color were dingy with age.

A warped wooden dresser sat against the wall opposite the bed. It leaned to one side. The drawers hung out.

A bed. A lamp. A dresser.

Only three pieces of furniture in this huge, windowless room.

Even the walls were bare. Not a single picture covered the dreary gray paint.

I sat down on the bed. I leaned against the bars of the iron headboard.

I ran my fingers over the blanket. Scratchy wool. Scratchy wool that smelled of mothballs.

"No way I'm going to use that blanket," I said out loud. "No way." But I knew I would. The room was cold and damp, and I began to shiver.

I quickly changed into my pajamas and pulled the smelly old blanket over me.

I twisted and turned. Trying to get comfortable on the lumpy mattress.

I stared up at the ceiling and listened. Listened to the night sounds of the creepy old house. Strange creaking noises that echoed through the old walls.

Then I heard the howls.

Frightening animal howls on the other side of the wall.

The sad howls from the swamp.

I sat up.

Were they coming from Clark's room?

6

I listened hard, afraid to move.

Another long, sad howl. From outside. Not from Clark's room.

"Stop it!" I scolded myself. "Clark is the one with the wild imagination. Not you!"

But I couldn't shut out the eerie howls from the swamp.

Was it an animal? Was it a swamp monster?

I pressed the pillows over my face. It took me hours to fall asleep.

When I woke up, I didn't know if it was morning — or the middle of the night. Without a window, it was impossible to tell.

I read my watch — 8:30. Morning.

I searched through the suitcase for my new pink T-shirt. I needed something to cheer me up — and pink is my favorite color. I pulled on my jeans. Slipped on my muddy sneakers.

I dressed quickly. The room reminded me of a prison cell. I wanted to escape fast.

I opened the bedroom door and peeked into the hall.

Empty.

But there, across from my room, I saw a small window. I hadn't noticed it the night before.

A bright ray of sunshine filtered through the dusty glass. I peered outside — into the swamp.

A heavy mist hung over the red cypress trees, casting a soft, rosy glow over the wet land. The glowing mist made the swamp look mysterious and unreal.

Something purple fluttered on a nearby tree limb. A purple bird. A purple bird with a bright orange beak. I'd never seen a bird like that before.

Then I heard the sounds again.

The horrible howls. The shrill cries.

From animals hiding deep in the swamp — all kinds of creatures I'd probably never seen before.

Swamp creatures.

Swamp monsters.

I shuddered. Then turned away from the window and headed for Clark's room.

I knocked on the door. "Clark!"

No answer.

"Clark?"

Silence.

I burst through the door and let out a cry.

The sheets on Clark's bed lay in a tangled

29

mess — as if there had been some kind of struggle.

And now there was nothing left of Clark — nothing but part of his pajamas, crumpled on the bed!

7

"Noooo!"

I opened my mouth in a terrified cry.

"Gretchen — what's your problem?"

Clark stepped out from the closet.

He wore a T-shirt, baseball cap, sneakers, and his pajama bottoms.

"Uh . . . n-no problem," I stammered, my heart still pounding.

"Then why did you scream?" Clark demanded. "And why do you look so weird?"

"*I* look weird? You're the one who looks weird," I snapped. I pointed to his pajama bottoms. "Where are your pants?"

"I don't know." He shook his head. "I think Mom must have packed them in your suitcase by mistake."

I have to stop letting this big, old house spook me. Clark is the one with the wild imagination — not me, I reminded myself again.

"Come on," I told my stepbrother. "Let's go back to my room and look for your jeans."

On the way down to breakfast, Clark stopped to peer out the hall window. The mist had cleared. The dew-covered plants glistened in the sunlight.

"It looks sort of pretty, doesn't it?" I murmured.

"Yeah," Clark replied. "Pretty. Pretty creepy."

The kitchen looked pretty creepy too. It was dark — almost as dark in the morning as the night before. But the back door was open and some sun splashed on the floor and the walls.

We could hear the sounds of the swamp through the open door. But I tried to ignore them.

Grandma stood by the stove, a spatula in one hand, a huge plate of blueberry pancakes in the other. She set down the spatula and plate and wiped her hands on her faded flower apron. Then she gave us each a big good-morning hug — smearing Clark with pancake batter.

I pointed at the stains on his shirt and giggled. Then I glanced down at my shirt. My brand-new pink T-shirt. Splotched with blueberry stains.

I glanced around the kitchen for something to use to clean my shirt. The room was a disaster.

Globs of pancake batter dripped from the stove. Batter covered the countertops and stuck to the floor.

Then I took a good look at Grandma. She was a disaster too.

Her face was striped — blue and white. Flour and blueberry stains filled the creases of her wrinkled cheeks. She had flour streaked across her nose and chin.

"Did you sleep well?" She smiled, and her blue eyes crinkled. With the back of her hand, she wiped a wisp of gray hair from her eyes. Now a glob of blueberry batter nested in the thin strands of her hair.

"I did," Grandpa answered, as a loud shriek rang out from the swamp. "Always do. It's so quiet and peaceful here."

I had to smile. Maybe Grandpa is lucky that he's hard-of-hearing, I thought.

Grandpa headed out the door, and Clark and I brushed ourselves off. Then we took our seats at the table.

In the middle of the table sat another plate of blueberry pancakes. This plate was even bigger than the one Grandma had been holding. And it was stacked high with blueberry pancakes.

"Grandma must think we eat like pigs," Clark leaned over and whispered. "There's enough here for fifty people."

"I know," I groaned. "And we'll have to eat them all. Otherwise, she'll be insulted."

"We do?" Clark gulped.

That's one of the things I really like about my stepbrother. He believes almost everything I tell him.

"Help yourself," Grandma chirped, carrying two more plates of pancakes to the table. "Don't be shy."

Why did Grandma make all these pancakes? I wondered. *There's no way we could eat all of them. No way.*

I placed a few pancakes on my plate. Grandma heaped about ten onto Clark's plate. His face turned green.

Grandma sat down with us. But her plate remained empty. She didn't take a single pancake.

All those pancakes and she didn't even take one. I don't get it, I thought. *I just don't get it.*

"What's that you're reading, dear?" She pointed to Clark's rolled-up comic, sticking out of the back pocket of his jeans.

"*Creatures from the Muck,*" he answered between bites.

"Oh, how interesting," Grandma replied. "I love to read. So does Grandpa Eddie. We read all the time. We love mysteries. 'There's nothing like a good mystery,' Grandpa Eddie always says."

I jumped up from the table. I just remembered — Grandma and Grandpa's presents were still packed in my suitcase.

Books! Mysteries! Dad told us they loved them.

"Be right back!" I excused myself and dashed upstairs.

I started down the long, winding hall to my room. Then stopped when I heard footsteps.

Who could it be?

I gazed down the dark hall. I gasped when I spotted a shadow moving against the wall.

Someone else was up here.

Someone was creeping toward me.

8

I pressed my back against the wall. Held my breath and listened.

The shadow slid out of view.

The footsteps grew softer.

Still holding my breath, I inched down the dark twisting hallway. I peeked around a corner. And saw it.

The shadow. Nearly shapeless in the dim light.

It moved slowly along the dark green walls, growing smaller as the footsteps faded in the distance.

I crept swiftly but silently, chasing the shadow through the corridor.

Whose shadow is it? I wondered. Who else is up here?

I crept closer.

The shadow on the wall loomed large again.

My heartbeat quickened as I chased the mysterious shape.

The shadow turned another corner. I hurried to the turn as quietly as I could. And stopped.

Whoever it was — stood right there. Just beyond the turn.

I took a deep breath — and peeked around the corner.

And saw Grandpa Eddie.

Grandpa Eddie — carrying a huge platter stacked high with blueberry pancakes.

How did Grandpa get up here? I wondered. I thought I saw him go outside.

Grandpa came in through another door, I decided. That has to be it. This house is huge. It probably has lots of doors and halls and stairways I haven't discovered yet.

But what was he doing up here carrying an enormous tray of pancakes? Where was he taking them?

What a mystery!

Grandpa Eddie carefully balanced the big silver tray between his hands as he made his way down the hall.

I have to follow him, I thought. I have to see where he's going.

I padded down the hallway. I wasn't too worried about being quiet now. After all, Grandpa didn't hear too well.

I walked only a few yards behind him.

When I heard the sounds, I froze.

Sniffing. Behind me. Furious sniffing.

Oh, no! Charley!

Charley bounded down the hall toward me. Sniffing. Sniffing furiously. Then the dog spotted me — and stopped.

"Good dog," I whispered, trying to shoo him away. "Go back. Go back."

But he broke into a run. Barking his head off.

I grabbed for his collar as he tried to dodge me — to race down the hall to Grandpa.

I grasped the collar tightly. He barked even louder.

"Rose?" Grandpa Eddie called out. "Is that you, Rose?"

"Come on, Charley," I whispered. "Let's get out of here."

I dragged Charley around the corner — before Grandpa could catch me spying on him. Tugging the dog, I ducked into my room.

I sat down on the scratchy blanket for a second to catch my breath. Then I quickly rummaged through my suitcase for Grandma and Grandpa's mystery books.

Where was Grandpa going with those pancakes? I wondered as I hurried down the stairs with the presents.

Why was he creeping along so silently?

It was a mystery I had to solve.

If only I had minded my own business. . . .

9

"Why don't you two go out and play while I clean up these dishes?" Grandma suggested after breakfast. "Then you can help me make my sweet-as-sugar rhubarb pie!"

"Play?" Clark grumbled. "Does she think we're two years old?"

"Let's go out, Clark." I pulled him through the back door. Hanging out in a swamp wasn't exactly my idea of fun. But anything was better than sitting around that creepy old house.

We stepped into the bright sunlight — and I gasped. The hot, steamy air felt like a heavy weight against my skin. I tried to breathe deeply — to shake the smothered feeling I had.

"So what are we going to do?" Clark grumbled, also drawing in a deep breath.

I glanced around and spotted a path. It started at the back of the house and trailed into the swamp.

"Let's explore a little," I suggested.

"I am *not* walking through a swamp," Clark declared. "No way."

"What are you afraid of? Comic-book monsters?" I teased him. "Creatures from the muck?" I laughed.

"You're a riot," Clark muttered, scowling.

We walked a few steps. The sun filtered through the treetops, casting leafy shadows along the trail.

"Snakes," Clark admitted. "I'm afraid of snakes."

"Don't worry," I told him. "I'll watch out for snakes. You watch out for gators."

"Gators?" Clark's eyes opened wide.

"Yeah, sure," I replied. "Swamps are filled with man-eating alligators."

A voice interrupted us. "Gretchen. Clark. Don't stray too far."

I turned and saw Grandpa. He stood a few yards behind us.

What was that in his hand?

A huge saw. Its sharp teeth glinted in the sunlight.

Grandpa headed toward a small, unfinished shed. It stood a few feet off the side of the path, tucked between two tall cypress trees.

"Okay!" I shouted to Grandpa. "We won't go far."

"Want to help finish the shed?" he yelled, waving the saw. "Building things builds confidence, I always say!"

"Um, maybe later," I answered.

"Want to help?" Grandpa shouted again.

Clark cupped his hands around his mouth and yelled, "LA-TER!" Then he turned back toward the path.

And tripped.

Over a dark form that rose up quickly, silently from the muddy grass.

10

"Gator! Gator!" Clark shrieked.

Grandpa waved his saw wildly. "Later? Later? Okay!"

"Help me! Help me! It's got me!" Clark wailed.

I peered down.

Down at the dark shape in the grass.

And laughed.

"Cypress knee," I said calmly.

Clark turned, his mouth still open in fright. He stared at the knobby form in the grass.

"It's a cypress limb, poking up from the grass," I explained. "It's called a cypress knee. I showed you one yesterday. Remember?"

"I remembered!" he lied. "I just wanted to scare you."

I started to crack a joke, but I saw Clark's whole body trembling as he picked himself up. I felt kind of sorry for him. "Let's go back to the house," I suggested. "Grandma is probably waiting for us. To make her sweet-as-sugar rhubarb pie."

On the way back, I told Clark about seeing Grandpa upstairs, and the huge tray of pancakes he carried. But Clark didn't think it was all that strange.

"He probably likes to eat in bed," he said. "Mom and Dad always like breakfast in bed."

"Yeah, maybe," I agreed. But I wasn't convinced. I wasn't convinced at all.

"Well, you two look as if you've had fun!" Grandma chirped when we walked through the door.

Clark and I glanced at each other and shrugged.

"Are you ready to bake?" Grandma smiled. "Everything is ready." She waved at the counter, at the pie ingredients all lined up.

"Who wants to roll out the dough," she asked, staring straight at me, "while I slice the rhubarb?"

"I guess I will," I replied.

Clark sighed. "Uh, maybe I'll go into the living room and read my comic," he told Grandma, trying to escape. "Mom says I just get in the way when she cooks."

"Nonsense!" Grandma replied. "You measure out the sugar. Lots and lots of sugar."

I rolled out the pie dough. It seemed like an awful lot of dough. But then — what did I know? I'm never around when Mom bakes. She says I get in the way too.

When the dough was rolled flat, Grandma took

over. "Okay, children. You sit down at the table and have a nice glass of milk. I'll finish up."

Clark and I weren't thirsty. But we didn't feel like arguing. We drank our milk and watched Grandma finish making the pie.

No — not one pie. *Three* pies.

"Grandma, how come you're making *three* pies?" I asked.

"I always like to have a little extra," she explained. "Just in case company drops in."

Company? I thought. Company?

I stared at Grandma.

Is she totally losing it?

Who did she think was coming to visit? She lives in the middle of nowhere!

What is going on around here? I wondered.

Is Grandma really expecting visitors?

Why does she make so much extra food?

11

"Work builds thirst!" Grandpa announced, banging open the kitchen door. He headed for the refrigerator. "See! I'm right!" Grandpa pointed to our empty milk glasses. "Are you two ready to help with the shed now?"

"Eddie, the children didn't come here to work!" Grandma scolded. "Why don't you two have some fun exploring the house? There are endless rooms. I'm sure you'll find some wonderful treasures."

"Great idea!" Grandpa's face lit up with a smile. But it faded quickly. "Just one warning. You'll find a locked room. At the end of the hall on the third floor. Now pay attention, children. Stay away from that room."

"Why? What's in it?" Clark demanded.

Grandma and Grandpa exchanged worried glances. Grandma's face turned bright pink.

"It's a supply room," Grandpa replied. "We've stored away things in there. Old things. Fragile things. Things that could easily break. So just stay away."

Clark and I took off. We were glad to get away. Grandma Rose and Grandpa Eddie were nice — but weird.

The kitchen, living room, and dining room took up most of the first floor. And we'd seen them already.

There was a library on the first floor too. But the books in there were old and dusty. They made me sneeze. Nothing very exciting in there. So Clark and I headed upstairs. To the second floor.

We made our way past our bedrooms.

Past the little hall window.

We followed the twists and turns of the dim hallway — until we came to the next room.

Grandma and Grandpa's bedroom.

"I don't think we should go in there," I told Clark. "I don't think Grandma and Grandpa want us snooping through their things."

"Come on!" he urged. "Don't you want to check it out? For pancake crumbs." He laughed.

I shoved Clark hard.

"Hey!" he grumbled. His glasses slid down his nose. "It was just a joke."

I left my stepbrother in the hall and opened the door to the next room. The door was made of heavy, dark wood. It groaned when I pushed it.

I fumbled in the dark for the light switch. The

room glowed a sickly yellow — from a single, dirty bulb, dangling from the ceiling.

In the dreary light, I could make out cartons. A room full of cartons. Stacks and stacks of them.

"Hey! Maybe there's some cool stuff in these boxes," Clark said, pushing past me.

Clark began to pry one open. "Whatever is in here must be pretty big," he said, pointing to the carton's bulging sides.

I peered over Clark's shoulder. The room smelled so musty and sour. I held my nose and squinted in the dim light. Waiting for Clark to reveal what was inside the box.

Clark struggled with the cardboard flaps — and finally they sprang open.

"I don't believe this!" he exclaimed.

"What?" I demanded, craning my neck. "What?"

"Newspapers. Old newspapers," Clark reported.

We lifted the top layers of newspapers to reveal — more newspapers. Old, yellowed newspapers.

We opened five more boxes.

Newspapers.

All the cartons were stuffed with newspapers. A room filled with cartons and cartons of newspapers. Dating way back to before Dad was born. More than fifty years of newspapers.

Why would anyone want to save all this stuff? I wondered.

"Whoa!" Clark leaned over a box across the room. "You're not going to believe what's in this one!"

"What? What's in it?"

"Magazines." Clark grinned.

My brother was starting to get on my nerves. But I made my way across the room. I liked magazines. Old ones and new ones.

I shoved my hand deep inside the magazine box and lifted out a stack.

I felt something tickle the palm of my hand. Under the magazines.

I peeked underneath.

And screamed.

12

Hundreds of cockroaches skittered through my fingers.

I flung the magazines to the floor.

I shook my hand hard, trying to shake the ugly brown bugs off. "Help me!" I wailed. "Get them off me!"

I felt prickly legs scurrying up my arm.

I struggled to brush them off — but there were dozens of them!

Clark grabbed a magazine from the floor and tried to swat them off. But as he whacked my arm, *more* roaches flew out from the pages.

Onto my T-shirt. My neck. My face!

"Ow! Nooo!" I shrieked. "Help me! Help me!"

I felt a cockroach skitter across my chin.

I brushed it off — and slapped one off my cheek.

Frantic, I grabbed Clark's comic from his back pocket — and began batting at the scurrying cockroaches. Brushing and batting. Brushing and batting.

"Gretchen! Stop!" I heard Clark scream. "Stop! They're all off. Stop!"

Gasping for breath, I peered down.

He was right. They were gone.

But my body still itched. I wondered if I would itch forever.

I went out into the hall and sat on the floor. I had to wait for my heart to stop pounding before I could speak. "That was so gross," I finally moaned. "Totally gross."

"Tell me about it." Clark sighed. "Did you have to use my comic?" He held it up by a corner. Not sure if it was safe to stuff back in his pocket.

My skin still felt as if prickly roach legs were crawling all over it. I shuddered — and brushed myself off one last time.

"Okay." I stood up and peered down the dreary hallway. "Let's see what's in the next room."

"Really?" Clark asked. "You really want to?"

"Why not?" I told him. "I'm not afraid of little bugs. Are you?"

Clark hated bugs. I knew he did. Big ones *and* little ones. But he wouldn't admit it. So he led the way into the next room.

We pushed open the heavy door — and peered inside.

13

"Wow! Look at all this junk!" My stepbrother stood in the middle of the room. Spinning round and round. Taking it all in.

A room filled with toys and games. Really old toys and games. Mountains of them.

In one corner stood a rusty tricycle. The big front tire was missing.

"I bet this belonged to Dad," I said. It was hard to imagine Dad as a little kid, riding this trike.

I honked the horn. It still worked.

Clark pulled out a dusty chess set from a banged-up wooden box. He began setting up the board while I hunted through the rest of the junk.

I found a teddy bear with its head badly twisted out of shape.

A box that held a single roller skate.

A stuffed toy monkey with one of its arms yanked off.

I rummaged through bags and bags of little toy

soldiers, their uniforms faded, their faces rubbed off.

Then I spotted an antique toy chest. It had a golden carousel painted on it, dulled with age.

I lifted the dusty lid. A porcelain doll rested face down inside the chest.

I lifted her gently. And turned her face toward me.

Fine cracks ran across her delicate cheeks. A small chip marred the tip of her nose.

Then I stared into her eyes — and gasped.

She had no eyes.

No eyes at all.

Just two black holes cut out of the space below her small forehead. Two gaping black holes.

"*These* are Grandma's treasures?" I croaked. "It's all junk!"

I dropped the doll into the chest.

And heard a squeak.

From the other side of the room. Next to the door.

I turned and saw a rocking horse, rocking back and forth.

"Clark, did you push that horse?" I demanded.

"No," Clark replied, softly, watching the horse rock back and forth. Back and forth. Squeaking.

"Let's get out of here," I said. "This room is starting to give me the creeps."

"Me, too," Clark said. "Someone beheaded the

queen in the chess set. Chewed her head right off."

Clark leaped over some boxes and jumped into the hall.

I turned for one last look before I clicked off the light. *Totally creepy*.

"Clark?"

Where did he go?

I glanced up and down the long hall.

No sign of him. But he was just there. Standing in the doorway.

"Clark? Where are you?"

I walked down the corridor, following its twists and turns.

A queasy feeling settled in my stomach. My heart began to race.

"Clark? This isn't funny."

No answer.

"Clark? Where *are* you?"

14

"BOOOOOO!"

I let out a long shrill scream.

Clark stepped out from behind me, bent over with laughter. "Gotcha!" he cried. "Gotcha big-time!"

"That wasn't funny, Clark," I growled at him. "It was just dumb. I wasn't even scared."

He rolled his eyes. "Why can't you just admit it, Gretchen? Admit it — just once. You were totally scared."

"*Not!*" I insisted. "You just surprised me. That's all." I stuffed my hands in my jeans pockets so Clark wouldn't see them shaking. "You're a real jerk," I told him.

"Well, Grandma told us to have fun. And *that* was fun!" he teased. "So where should we go now?"

"*We* aren't going anywhere," I told him angrily. "I'm going to hide in my room and read."

"Hey! Great idea!" Clark exclaimed. "Let's play hide-and-seek!"

"*Play?* Did I hear you say *play?*" I asked sarcastically. "I thought you said that only two-year-olds *play.*"

"This is different," Clark explained. "Hide-and-seek in this house is definitely not for babies."

"Clark, I am not — "

He didn't let me finish. "NOT IT!" he cried. Then he took off, running down the hall to hide.

"I don't want to be It," I grumbled. "I don't want to play hide-and-seek."

Okay, I told myself. Get this over with. Find Clark fast. Then you can go to your room and read.

I started to count by fives.

"Five, ten, fifteen, twenty . . ." I called out, counting to one hundred. Then I started down the dark hall. When I reached the end, the hall turned — revealing an old winding staircase that led up to the third floor.

I started to climb the dusty, wooden stairs. They wound round and round. I looked up ahead, but I couldn't see where the steps led.

I couldn't even see my own feet. It was totally black in there.

The stairs creaked and groaned with every step I took. A thick layer of grime coated the banister — but I held onto it anyway. And I groped my way up — up the dark, winding staircase.

Breathing hard, I climbed higher and higher. The dust in the air stuck in my throat. It smelled sour and old.

I finally reached the top of the staircase and peered down the third-floor hallway. It looked like the one below — with the same twists and turns.

The same dark green walls. The same dim shaft of light that entered from a single window.

I slowly moved down the hall and opened the first door I reached.

It was a huge room. Almost as big as the living room. But totally empty.

The next room was just as large. Just as empty.

I moved carefully down the dark hall.

It was really hot up here. Beads of sweat dripped down the sides of my face. I blotted them with the sleeve of my T-shirt.

The next room I entered was small. Well, not exactly small, but the smallest I'd seen so far. Against one wall stood an old player piano.

If it wasn't so gross up here, I'd come back to this room, I thought. I'd come back and see if the old piano worked.

But right now all I wanted to do was find Clark in his hiding place. And leave.

I walked a little farther.

Rounded a corner.

And choked on a scream — as I started to fall.
No floor!
No floor at all beneath my feet!
My hand shot out in the dark, fumbling for something to grab onto.
I grabbed something hard — an old banister.
And held on. Held on. Held on.
I gripped it tightly with both hands and swung myself back. Back up to the solid hallway floor.
My heart pounding, I stared down into the gaping black hole where I had fallen. A hole where an old staircase once stood. Now rotted away with age.
I let out a long sigh. "I'll get you for this, Clark," I cried out loud. "I told you I didn't want to play."
I hurried down the hall, searching for my stepbrother. Searching quickly. To get this dumb game over with.
And then I stopped.
And stared — at the door at the end of the hall.
A door with a shiny metal lock.
I moved slowly toward the door. A tarnished silver key rested in the keyhole.
What is inside there? I wondered. Why is it locked?
I stepped closer.
Why don't Grandma and Grandpa want us in that room?
They said it was a supply room.

Practically every room in this weird old house is a storage room, I thought. Why don't they want us to open *that* door?

I stood in front of the door.

I reached out my hand.

And wrapped my fingers around the silver key.

15

No.

I pulled my hand away from the doorknob.

I have to find Clark, I decided. I'm tired of playing this stupid game. I'm tired of being It.

Then I had a great idea.

I'll hide! I'll trick Clark into being It!

I'll hide and Clark will get bored waiting for me to find him. He'll have to look for me!

Perfect! I thought. Now . . . where shall I hide?

I searched the rest of the rooms on the third floor — scouting out a good hiding place. But the rooms up here were all empty. Nothing to slip behind.

Nothing to crawl under.

I returned to the little room with the player piano. Maybe I can figure out a way to hide behind that, I thought.

I tried to push the piano away from the wall.

Just enough so I could squeeze behind it. But it was way too heavy. I couldn't budge it.

I made my way back to the door with the silver key — the locked room.

I peered up and down the dim hall. Had I searched everywhere? Did I miss a room?

That's when I spotted it.

A small door. A door in the wall.

A door I hadn't noticed before.

A door to a dumbwaiter.

I'd seen dumbwaiters in the movies. In big, old houses like this one. They were little elevators that carried food and dishes from one floor to another. Pretty cool.

A dumbwaiter! I thought. A perfect place to hide! I turned and started toward it — when I heard a crash. A crash — like the sound of a plate dropping.

A crash coming from the other side of the door with the silver key.

I pressed my ear against the door. I heard footsteps.

So *that's* where Clark is hiding! I realized. He is such a cheater! He hid in the one place he knew I wouldn't look!

He hid in the room Grandma and Grandpa told us to stay out of.

Well, Clark, I thought. Too bad for you. I found you!

I slipped my fingers around the key and turned it. The lock sprang open with a sharp click. I yanked open the door.

And stared at a hideous monster.

16

I nearly fell into the room.

I couldn't move. Couldn't back away. Couldn't take my eyes off him.

A living, breathing monster. At least ten feet tall. Standing inside the locked room.

I gaped at his big, furry body. A body like a gorilla — with leaves and tree roots and sand tangled in his fur. His head was scaly, with snapping rows of jagged alligator teeth.

A foul stench filled the room. The putrid smell of decay. The smell of the swamp.

My stomach heaved.

The creature raised his eyes to me — bulging eyes set into the sides of his enormous head.

He held me in his stare for a moment. Then he glanced down at his hairy paws — where he balanced a tall stack of pancakes.

He began stuffing the pancakes into his mouth. Devouring them. Gnashing them with his jagged teeth.

Still gripping the door handle, I stared at the monster as he ate. He jammed another stack of pancakes down his throat. He swallowed them whole and grunted with pleasure.

His horrible alligator eyes went wide. The thick veins in his neck throbbed as he ate.

I tried to call for help. To scream. But when I opened my mouth, no sound came out.

With one hand the monster shoved pancakes into his mouth — stacks at a time. With the other, he scratched at one of his furry legs.

Scratched and scratched. Until he found a big black beetle, nesting in his fur.

He held the beetle up to the side of his head — to one of his bulging eyes.

The beetle's legs waved in the air.

He glared at the beetle. At the waving legs.

Then he popped the bug into his mouth — and chomped down on its shiny black shell with a sickening crunch.

Blueberries and beetle juice oozed from his mouth.

Run! I told myself. *Run!* But I was too terrified to move.

The creature reached down for another stack of pancakes.

I forced myself to take a small step back — into the hall.

The monster jerked his head up.

He glared at me. Then he let out a deep growl.

He let the pancakes slide to the floor and lumbered toward me.

I ran, screaming for help as I charged into the hall.

"Gretchen! Gretchen! What's wrong?" Clark turned the corner at the end of the corridor.

"A monster! In the locked room! Hurry!" I shrieked. "Hurry! Get help!"

I leaped down the stairs. "Grandma! Grandpa!" I cried out. "A monster!"

I turned to see if the beast was following me — and realized that Clark hadn't moved.

"There's a monster in there!" I wailed. "Get away, Clark! Get away!"

He snickered. "You must think I'm pretty stupid to fall for that one."

Clark headed toward the door of the monster's room. Grinning.

"No! Please!" I pleaded. "I'm telling the truth!"

"You just want to scare me. To get even."

"I'm not kidding, Clark! Don't go in there!" I shrieked. "DON'T!"

Clark reached the door. "Here I am, swamp monster!" he called out as he stepped into the room. "Come and get me!"

17

A second later Clark's terrified screams echoed from the room.

The creature roared over Clark's cries.

Charley bounded up the stairs, barking wildly.

"Run! Run!" Clark came bursting from the room, waving his arms. "A monster! A swamp monster!"

We tore down the stairs, dragging Charley with us. Charley fought hard. He wanted to turn around and charge back up the steps.

"Charley, come!" I pleaded. "Come!"

But Charley sat down on a step and howled. He wouldn't budge.

A bellow thundered through the hall.

Oh, no! He's coming! He's coming after us!

"PLEASE, CHARLEY!" I begged, yanking on his collar. "PLEASE!"

Clark stood on the steps, frozen in fear.

"Help me, Clark!" I pleaded. "Don't just stand there. Help me!"

The swamp monster pounded down the hall. The old stairway quaked under our feet.

"He's coming to get us," Clark whispered. He still hadn't moved.

I grabbed my stepbrother's T-shirt and yanked him hard. "Help me, Clark!" I screamed. "Push Charley!"

We struggled down the stairs. I tugged Charley and Clark shoved him from behind.

"Grandma! Grandpa!" I cried out.

No answer.

The monster's roar grew louder. Closer.

"Lock Charley in the bathroom!" I ordered Clark when we reached the second floor. "He'll be safe there. I'll find Grandma and Grandpa."

I charged down to the kitchen. "Grandma! Grandpa!" I yelled. "A monster!"

No one in the kitchen.

I flew into the living room. "Where are you? Help!"

Not in the living room.

I searched the library. Empty.

I ran back up the stairs. I checked their bedroom and all the other rooms on the second floor.

I couldn't find them anywhere.

Where are they? Where could they be? I asked myself.

Clark stepped out of the bathroom — just in time to hear the monster's footsteps rumbling above us.

"W-where's Grandma and Grandpa?" he stammered.

"I — I don't know. I can't find them!"

"Did you check outside?" His voice came out in a squeak.

That's it! I thought. Don't panic, Gretchen. They must be outside. Probably in the back. Grandpa is probably working on the shed.

We bolted down the stairs and into the kitchen.

We stopped at the back door. Stared out across the swamp. To the shed.

No one back there.

"Where are — ?" Clark began.

"Listen!" I cut Clark off. "Do you hear that?"

The sound of a car — starting up.

"Grandpa and Grandma's car! It's back! It's fixed!" I shouted.

We followed the sound of the engine. It was coming from the front of the house.

We ran to the front door and peered out the window.

There they were!

"Huh?" I cried out in shock.

My grandparents were backing down the driveway.

They were driving away!

"No — wait! Wait!" I screamed, turning the lock.

"They can't hear you!" Clark shouted. "Open the door! Open it!"

I yanked on the door. I pulled it as hard as I could. I turned the lock again.

"Hurry!" Clark shrieked. "They're leaving us here!"

I tugged and tugged. And turned the knob frantically.

Then I realized the horrible truth.

"It's bolted from the outside!" I told Clark. "They've locked us in!"

18

"How could they do this to us?" I wailed. "How could they leave us here? Why did they lock us in?"

The ceiling shook above our heads. Shook hard. Hard enough to send the pictures on the living-room wall crashing to the floor.

"What was that?" Clark's eyebrows shot up.

"The monster! He's coming after us!" I croaked. "We have to get out of here! We have to find help!"

Clark and I ran back to the kitchen. To the kitchen door.

I twisted the doorknob. Pulled as hard as I could. But this door was also jammed shut — barred from the outside.

We ran through the house.

We checked all the side doors.

All stuck. All of them — bolted shut from the other side.

The monster's footsteps rumbled above us.

How could Grandma and Grandpa do this to

us? How could they? How could they? The question screamed in my head as I charged into the library. To the window.

The only window on the entire first floor.

Our only escape now.

I struggled to shove the window up.

It wouldn't budge.

I pounded on the wooden sash with my fists.

"Look!" Clark choked. He pointed to the grimy pane. "Look!"

Two rusty nails. Driven into the wooden sash. Nailing the window shut — from the outside.

Nailing us in.

How could they do this to us? How could they? I chanted silently. *How could they?*

"We have to break the glass!" I turned to Clark. "It's the only way out!"

"Okay!" Clark cried. He leaned forward and began beating his fists against the pane.

"Are you nuts?" I screamed at him. "Find something stronger to — "

But the rest of my sentence was lost — lost in a deafening crash from above. Followed by the thundering clatter of piano keys.

"Wh-what's he doing?" Clark stammered.

"There's an old piano up there. It sounds as if he's throwing it across the room!"

The floors, the walls, the library ceiling — everything quaked — as the monster hurled the piano across the third-floor room. Over and over again.

A porcelain vase, a crystal dish, little glass animals flew from a nearby table and shattered at our feet.

I threw my hands over my head as the library books spilled from their shelves.

Clark and I huddled together. On the floor. Waiting for the avalanche of books to end.

Waiting for the monster to stop.

We huddled there until the house grew silent.

A final book tumbled from a shelf. It landed on a small table next to me.

"Hand me that!" I ordered Clark, pointing to a heavy brass candlestick next to the book. "Stand back."

I turned to the window. I pulled back my arm to swing the heavy candlestick — when I heard the whimpering.

Charley's whimpering. From upstairs.

"Oh, no!" I gasped. "The monster — he's got Charley!"

19

I ran for the stairway, clutching the candlestick in one hand, dragging Clark with the other.

I had to save Charley! I had to!

I raced up the stairs. I stopped when I reached the top.

My heart pounded in my chest as I peered down the hall.

The corridor was empty.

I crept toward the bathroom. Except for Clark's raspy breathing and the thudding of my heart, the house was still.

As I neared the bathroom, the bathroom door came into view.

Shut.

I gripped the doorknob. It slipped in my sweat-drenched hand.

I opened the door a crack and peeked inside. But I couldn't see anything.

I could feel Clark breathing down my neck as I pushed the door open a bit more.

A bit more.

"Charley!" I cried out with relief.

Charley sat in the bathtub. Curled up in a corner. Scared — but safe.

He gazed up at us with his big brown eyes. He wagged his tail weakly. Then he began to bark.

"Shhhh!" I whispered, petting him. "Please, Charley. Don't let the monster hear you. Quiet, boy."

Charley barked even louder.

So loud that we almost didn't hear the car pull up outside.

"Shhhh!" I urged Charley. I turned to Clark. "Did you hear that?"

His mouth dropped open. "A car door!"

"Yes!" I cried.

"Grandma and Grandpa are back!" Clark shouted. "I'll bet they brought help!"

"Stay," I commanded Charley as we eased out of the bathroom. "Good boy. Stay."

Clark slammed the door behind us, and we bolted down the stairs.

"I knew they'd be back! I knew they wouldn't just leave us!" I flew down the steps, two at a time.

And heard the engine start.

Heard the car rumble away.

Heard the tires crunch down the driveway.

"Noooo!" I shouted as I reached the front door. "Don't go! Don't go!"

I pounded the door with my fists. I kicked it hard. And then I saw the pink slip of paper on the floor, slipped under the door.

A message. I picked it up with a trembling hand. And started to read:

We're not coming back. Until next week. Sorry, kids. But work is taking much longer than we thought.

A phone message — from Mom and Dad.

Grandma and Grandpa didn't come back, I realized. Mr. Donner, from the general store, had driven over to deliver this phone message.

The roar of the monster tore through my thoughts.

I spun around.

Clark was gone.

"Clark!" I shouted. "Where are you?"

The monster's growls grew louder. Meaner.

"Clark!" I called out again. "Clark!"

"Gretchen — come quick!" I heard his desperate cry from the kitchen.

20

"Gretchen! Gretchen!"

As I charged through the living room, he shouted my name over and over again. Each time his voice grew higher, more excited.

"I'm coming!" I yelled. "Hold on, Clark. I'm coming!"

I rounded the couch — and tripped over a footstool. My head hit the floor hard.

Clark continued to cry out my name, but his voice seemed distant now. So far away.

My head throbbed with pain.

I struggled to stand, and the room spun around me.

"Gre-tchen! Gre-tchen!"

He sounded more frantic than ever.

"I'm coming!" I said through a dizzy haze.

Then I heard the monster's bellow. It thundered through the house.

I have to get to Clark. He's in trouble! The monster has him! I realized.

I stumbled through the living room. Toward the kitchen.

The creature's roars shook the walls.

"Hold on, Clark!" I tried to shout, but my voice came out in a moan. "I'm coming!"

I stumbled into the kitchen.

"Gretchen!" Clark stood next to the refrigerator.

Alone.

"Where is he?" I cried. My eyes darted around the room, searching for the monster.

"Wh-where's who?" Clark stammered.

"The monster!" I yelled.

"Upstairs," Clark replied, puzzled. "What took you so long to get here?"

Clark didn't wait for an answer. "Look at this." He pointed to the refrigerator. I turned and saw two letters stuck there with magnets.

"You were screaming like a *maniac* to show me that?" I shrieked. "I nearly killed myself! I thought the monster had grabbed you!"

Clark's hand trembled as he lifted the envelopes from the refrigerator. "It's two letters addressed to us. From Grandma and Grandpa."

I stared at the envelopes in Clark's hand. They were addressed to us, just as he said. And they were numbered, one and two.

"They left us letters?" I couldn't believe it.

Clark ripped open the first envelope. The paper shook in his hands as he began to read it to himself.

His eyes scanned the paper. He mumbled as he read. I couldn't understand what he was saying.

"Let me have that!" I reached out for the letter, but Clark jerked back. He held the paper tightly and continued to read.

"Clark, what does it say?" I demanded.

He ignored me. He pushed his glasses up on his nose and kept on reading. Mumbling.

I watched Clark as he read.

I watched his eyes move down the page.

I watched his eyes grow wide with horror.

21

"Clark!" I shouted impatiently. "What does it say?"

Clark began to read the letter out loud. " 'Dear Gretchen and Clark,' " he started. The paper fluttered between his trembling fingers.

" 'We're sorry to do this to you, but we had to leave. A few weeks ago, a swamp monster invaded our house. We captured it in the room upstairs. Then we didn't know what to do with it. We didn't have a car, so we couldn't get to a phone to call for help.

" 'We've lived in terror for the past few weeks. We were afraid to let the monster out. It's so loud and angry all the time. We know it would have killed us.' "

My knees started to wobble as Clark continued.

" 'We didn't want to tell your parents about the creature. If we did, they wouldn't have let you come. We don't get many visitors here. We wanted so much to see you. But I guess we were wrong. You should have gone to Atlanta with your mother and father. I guess we were wrong to let you stay.' "

"They guess they were wrong! *They guess!*" I shrieked. "Can you *believe* them?"

Clark peered up from the letter. His face was white. Even his freckles seemed to disappear. He shook his head, stunned.

Then he continued to read our grandparents' letter. " 'We've been feeding the creature, slipping food through an opening Grandpa sawed in the bottom of the door. The monster eats a lot. But we had to feed him. We were afraid not to.

" 'We know it's unfair to run off now. But we're just going for help. We'll be back — as soon as we can find someone. Someone who knows what to do with this horrible beast.

" 'Sorry, kids. We really are — but we had to bolt you inside the house. To make sure you didn't wander into the swamp by yourselves. It's not safe out there.' "

Were they for *real*?

"Not safe *out there!*" I cried. "They left us in this house with a killer monster — and they say it's not safe *out there*! They're both crazy, Clark. Totally crazy!"

Clark nodded and continued reading. " 'Sorry, kids. We really, really are sorry. But just remember one thing: You are perfectly safe as long as . . .' "

The monster upstairs let out a loud bellow. And Clark dropped the letter.

I watched in horror as it sailed through the air. Floated down to the floor.

And slid under the refrigerator.

"Get it, Clark!" I yelled. "Quick!"

Clark stretched out on the floor and shoved his fingers under the refrigerator. But his fingers only managed to brush the tip of the paper, shoving it back.

"Stop!" I yelled. "You're pushing it away!"

But Clark didn't listen.

He shoved his hand in deeper. Groping for the paper.

Pushing it back. Farther and farther.

Until we couldn't see it anymore.

"What did it say?" I hollered. "You read the letter! We're perfectly safe as long as . . . what?"

"I — I didn't get to that part," Clark stammered.

I wanted to strangle him.

I spun around. And frantically searched for something to slip under the refrigerator — to ease out the letter.

But I couldn't find anything slim enough or long enough. Everything was way too big to fit underneath.

Clark tore open the kitchen cabinets and drawers looking for something we could use.

The monster stomped on the floor above us.

The ceiling quaked.

A dish fell off the counter and shattered on the cold gray tiles. Shattered into a thousand tiny pieces.

"Oh, no," I moaned, staring up at the ceiling, watching the paint crack and crumble. "He's down to the second floor. He's coming closer."

"We're doomed," Clark groaned. "He's going to catch us and — "

"Clark. We have to move the refrigerator. We have to find out what it says in the rest of that letter!"

Clark and I tugged on the refrigerator. We pushed and tugged with all our strength.

Upstairs, the monster roared an angry roar.

We tugged harder.

The refrigerator began to move.

Clark knelt down and peered underneath it. "Push!" he told me. "Push! I can see a corner of the letter! Push — just a little more!"

I gave the refrigerator one more hard shove — and Clark had it! He grasped the corner of the letter between his thumb and index finger. And pulled it out.

He shook the paper, to free a clump of dust that clung to it.

"Just read it!" I shouted at him. "Read it!"

Clark started to read again. " 'You are perfectly safe as long as . . . ' "

22

I held my breath, waiting for Clark to finish the sentence. Waiting to find out how we could keep ourselves safe.

" 'You are perfectly safe,' " Clark read, " 'as long as you do not open the door and let the monster out.' "

"That's it?" My jaw dropped. "It's too late for that! It's too late! Did they say anything else? They must have said something else!"

"There's a little more." Clark read on:

" 'Please. Please stay away from that room. Do not open that door.' "

"Too late!" I wailed. "It's too late!"

" 'If the monster escapes, you will have no choice. You will have to find a way to kill it.' " Clark looked up from the letter. "That's it, Gretchen. That's all it says. *You will have to find a way to kill it.*"

"Quick!" I ordered Clark. "Open the other letter. It'll probably tell us more. It has to!"

Clark started to tear open the second envelope when we heard the heavy footsteps.

Footsteps downstairs.

In the next room — the living room.

"Hurry, Clark! Open it!"

Clark's fingers fumbled as he tried to rip through the sealed envelope. But he stopped when we heard the creature's breathing.

Deep, wheezing breaths.

Coming nearer.

My heart thumped wildly as the monster's wheezing grew louder.

"He–he's coming for us!" Clark cried, stuffing the unopened envelope in his pocket.

"The dining room!" I shouted. "Head for the dining room!"

"What are we going to do? How can we kill it?" Clark cried as we bolted from the kitchen.

"We — *owwww!*" A sharp pain shot up my leg as I ran smack into the dining-room table.

I clutched my knee. I tried to bend it. But the pain tore through it.

I spun around.

And there he stood.

The swamp monster.

In the kitchen — lumbering toward us hungrily.

23

The monster glared at me with his horrible bulging eyes. I watched the veins in his head throb as he let out a long, low growl.

I stared at those huge, pulsing veins. Stared as they beat against his coarse alligator skin.

"Run, Gretchen!" Clark pulled me from behind. He yanked me out of the dining room. We dove toward the stairs.

"We need a place to hide." Clark panted as we fled to the second floor. "We have to hide until Grandma and Grandpa come back with help."

"They're not coming back!" I screamed at him. "They're not coming back with help!"

"They said they would," Clark insisted. "They said so in the letter."

"Clark, you are such a jerk." We reached the top of the stairs. I stopped to catch my breath. "Who is going to believe them?" I said, gulping air. "Who's going to believe they have a swamp monster trapped in their house?"

Clark didn't reply.

I answered for him. "No one! That's who. Everyone they tell the story to will think they're nuts."

"Someone might believe them." Clark's voice cracked. "Someone might want to help."

"Yeah, right. *Will you help us kill a swamp monster?*' they'll ask. I'll bet they get loads of volunteers!" I rolled my eyes.

I stopped yelling at Clark when I heard the monster's heavy breathing. I spun around — and saw the creature.

He stood at the bottom of the stairs. Eyeing us. Drooling hungrily.

Clark and I backed slowly away from the top of the stairs.

The monster followed us with his eyes.

"We have to kill it," Clark whispered. "That's what the letter said. We have to kill it. But how?"

"I have an idea!" I told Clark. "Follow me!"

We turned and ran. As we charged past the bathroom, we heard Charley whimpering.

"Let's get Charley!" Clark stopped running. "It's too dangerous to leave him closed up in there. We have to take him with us."

"We can't, Clark," I replied. "He'll be okay. Don't worry."

I wasn't as sure about that as I sounded. But there was no time to stop for Charley now — because the monster had reached the second floor.

There he stood. Looming at the end of the hall.

He raised his hands up over his head. I saw that he held the wooden footstool I had tripped over in the living room.

His eyes burned with anger.

He glared at me, then growled a loud, savage growl. A stream of thick white drool dribbled down his chin.

He licked the drool away with a reptile tongue — and smashed the stool down across his leg. It splintered into two jagged pieces.

He raised the pieces and hurled them at us.

"Let's go!" Clark shrieked as the footstool bounced off the wall.

We ran up the stairs. Up to the third floor.

The monster lumbered after us. The whole house shook with each heavy step he took.

"He's coming!" Clark cried. "What are we going to do? You said you had an idea. What?"

"There's a collapsed stairway up here," I told Clark, running as fast as I could through the dark, twisting hall. "It's totally fallen down. Just a big hole. When we turn the corner, grab onto the railing. The monster will chase us around the corner — and he'll fall down the open stairway."

The roar of the monster thundered in my ears. I saw him plodding down the hall after us.

"Come on, Clark! Hurry!"

"What if it doesn't work?" Clark demanded,

very frightened. "What if the fall only *hurts* him? Won't it make him even more angry?"

"Don't ask questions, Clark," I replied impatiently. "It's got to work! It's got to!"

We started to run again.

The monster howled. Howled with rage.

"There's the turn, Clark. Up ahead."

The creature roared. Only steps behind us.

My heart pounded hard. My chest felt as if it were about to explode. "Grab the railing, Clark. Or else you'll drop to the bottom. Here goes!"

We turned the corner.

We both threw our hands up. And grabbed the railing.

Our bodies slammed hard against the wall — then dangled over the black, empty hole.

The creature turned the corner.

Would my plan work? Would he fall to his death? Was this the way to kill a monster?

24

The beast whirled around the corner.

Staggered on the edge of the hole.

His head jerked to face us. His eyes glowed red.

He opened his mouth in an ugly growl. He swayed, trying to keep his balance. Then he plunged down the open staircase.

I heard him land with a heavy thud.

Clark and I hung on to the rotted banister. It creaked under the strain of our weight.

My hands ached. My fingers were numb. I knew I couldn't hold on much longer.

We listened.

Silence.

The creature didn't move.

I looked down, but it was too dark to see.

"My fingers are slipping," Clark groaned. Then he swung out his foot, searching with his sneaker for the hallway floor.

Hand over hand, he inched his way along the banister to the safety of the hall. I followed.

We peered down into the black hole once more. But it was so black down there — we couldn't make out a thing. Dark and silent. Totally silent.

"We did it! We're safe!" I cheered. "We killed the monster!"

Clark and I jumped up and down in celebration. "We did it! We did it!"

We ran downstairs. We let Charley out of the bathroom.

"Everything is okay, Charley." I hugged my dog. "We did it, boy," I told him. "We killed the swamp monster."

"Let's get out of here," Clark urged. "We can walk to town. Call Mom and Dad from the general store. Tell them to pick us up — now!"

We were so happy, we practically danced down the steps. The three of us headed into the library. "Stand back," I told Clark. "And hold Charley. I'll break the window, and we'll get out of here."

I glanced around the room, searching for the heavy brass candlestick to break the glass. It wasn't there.

"Wait here," I told Clark. "I left the candlestick up in the bathroom. I'll be right back."

I sprinted out of the library.

I couldn't wait to break out of this creepy place. To leave this horrible swamp. And tell Mom and

Dad how stupid they were to dump us here in a house with a real, live monster inside.

I ran through the living room — to the stairs.

I jogged up three steps — and stopped.

Stopped when I heard the low groan.

It can't be, I thought. Maybe it's Charley. Maybe Charley is growling.

I listened.

And heard it again.

Not a dog growl. Definitely not a dog growl.

Then I heard the rumbling footsteps, the footsteps of the swamp monster, coming from somewhere nearby.

Closer.

Closer.

25

"Clark!" I staggered back into the library. My legs were shaking. My whole body trembled. "He's not dead!" I cried. "The monster isn't dead!"

The library was empty.

"Clark? Where are you?" I shouted.

"In the kitchen," he called. "Feeding Charley."

I raced into the kitchen. Clark and Charley sat on the floor. Charley was lapping up a bowl of water.

"The fall didn't kill him! The monster isn't dead!" I shrieked.

Clark gasped in horror. "He must be really angry now. He must be furious. What are we going to do?"

My eyes darted around the kitchen. "Put Charley in there," I ordered. "In that closet. I have another idea."

"I hope it's better than your last idea," Clark moaned.

"Do *you* have an idea?" I yelled at him. "Do you?"

He didn't.

Clark dragged Charley across the kitchen. "Gretchen, this isn't a closet. It's some kind of room."

"I don't care what it is," I hollered. "Just put Charley in there."

On the counter sat one of Grandma's rhubarb pies. "The monster hasn't eaten since this morning," I told Clark. "We'll put this pie out on the counter where he'll see it."

"But that will only slow him down for a second," Clark whined. He shut Charley in the room. "He'll gobble the pie in one bite. Then he'll come after us again."

"No, he won't," I insisted. "We're going to *poison* the pie. We'll put stuff in it. Enough stuff to kill him!"

"I don't know, Gretchen," Clark argued. "I don't think that's going to work."

Charley whimpered behind the closed door — as if he agreed.

"We have no choice!" I snapped. "We have to try *something*!"

I found a fork and carefully lifted up the pie crust with it.

Then I searched the cabinet under the kitchen sink. It was filthy under there. Damp, with green mold growing on the pipes.

92

I found a jar of turpentine sitting on a shelf right in front. The lid was screwed on tight. I had to twist it hard to open it.

I slowly poured the entire jar of turpentine into the pie.

"Yuck! That stuff stinks," Clark said, holding his nose.

I studied the pie. It was wet and runny now. "I think we need something to soak up the turpentine," I told Clark. "This should do it!" I held up a can of drain cleaner.

I sprinkled the blue drain-cleaner crystals over the pie. They made the rhubarb bubble and fizz.

Clark leaped back. "I think that's enough," he said.

I ignored him.

I stuck my head under the sink and came up with two jars. "Rat poison!" I exclaimed, reading the dirty label on one of them. "Excellent." The other jar was filled with ammonia.

"Hurry!" Clark urged. "I hear the monster. He's coming."

I sprinkled the pie with the rat poison and poured in the ammonia too.

The monster's groans came closer. Each time he groaned or growled, I jumped.

I found an old can of orange paint and dumped it into the pie.

"That's enough! We have enough!" Clark insisted in a panic.

"Okay. Okay. I just want to make sure this works."

I shoved in a handful of mothballs.

"Hurry!" Clark urged. "Close it up. He's coming!"

The monster's footsteps pounded the living-room floor.

"Hurry!" Clark begged.

I sprayed the top of the pie with bug spray.

"Gretchen!" Clark pleaded with me.

I placed the poisoned pie on the counter.

It's so sweet, your teeth will fall out after one bite. Grandma's words came back to me.

It better do more than that! I told myself. It better kill a monster!

"Here he comes!" Clark cried.

We ducked under the kitchen table.

The monster stomped into the kitchen. Peering out from under the table, I could see him swing his arms wildly. He knocked over dishes, pots, glasses. Everything in sight.

Then my heart stopped when I saw the big creature turn.

He hesitated. Then he took a step toward the kitchen table. Another step. Another.

Clark and I huddled together under the table. We were both trembling so hard, the table shook.

The swamp monster sees us under here! I realized.

We're trapped.

What is he going to do?

26

Clark and I held on to each other. The monster stepped up to the table — so close I could smell the sour odor of his·thick fur.

Clark started to let out soft, whimpering sounds.

I clapped my hands over his mouth. I shut my eyes.

Please go away, I prayed. Please, monster, don't *see* us.

I heard the creature sniffing. Like a dog trying to sniff out a bone.

When I opened my eyes, he had moved away from the table.

"Whew!" I breathed a long, silent sigh of relief.

The monster rumbled around the room.

Sniffing loudly, urgently.

He sniffed the refrigerator.

He lumbered over to the stove and sniffed some more. He plodded around the room. Sniffing.

He smells us. He smells Clark and me, I thought. *Please, see the pie. See the pie.*

The creature stomped back to the stove.

Sniffing.

He bent down and peered into the oven. Then he ripped the oven door off its hinges and hurled it across the room.

The door hit the wall with a loud crash. Clark jumped in fright and banged his head on the table. He let out a low moan.

I moaned too. "Look," I whispered.

The creature was eating — but he wasn't eating *our* pie. There were two pies still in the oven. And the creature was stuffing himself with them.

Oh, no, I thought. He'll eat those pies. Then he'll be full. He won't eat *our* pie! We're as good as dead.

The monster hungrily jammed the two pies into his mouth. He practically swallowed them whole. Then he lumbered to the center of the room.

Sniffing.

Yes! He's still hungry! I thought. *Eat our pie. Eat our pie,* I chanted to myself.

I peered out from under the table — and saw the creature, heading toward the counter. *Yes!*

He stopped.

And sniffed.

He saw the pie.

He eyed it for a moment. Then he lifted it to his mouth and shoved it in.

Yes! I cheered silently. *He's eating it! He's eating our pie!*

He chomped away at the pie. Chomped and shoved more into his huge mouth. Chomped and shoved. Chomped and shoved.

He licked his big lips as he ate.

He licked his paws.

He rubbed his stomach.

"Oh, no!" I groaned. "He *likes* it!"

27

I watched the monster shove the last bit of pie into his mouth.

Then he flicked his reptile tongue in and out, licking up every last crumb from the pie tin.

"It isn't working," I moaned to Clark. "He loves it."

"Now what are we going to do?" he whispered back. He hugged his knees tightly to his chest to keep them from shaking.

The monster let out a long groan.

I peered out from under the table. I saw the creature's eyes bug out. They practically popped out of his head!

A gurgling, choking sound escaped his throat.

He grasped his neck with his two hairy paws.

He groaned again.

His stomach rumbled — a deep rumble. He clutched his stomach and doubled over.

He uttered a weak cry of pain — and surprise.

Then he dropped dead on the kitchen floor.

"We did it! We did it!" I cheered. "We killed the swamp monster!"

I pulled Clark out from under the table.

I studied the creature from across the room. I was sure he was dead — but I still didn't want to get too close.

The monster's scaly eyelids were closed.

I stared at his chest — to see if it moved. To see if he was breathing.

His chest remained still.

I stared at him a few moments longer.

He didn't stir.

Clark peered over my shoulder. "Is — is he really dead?" he stammered.

"Yes!" I was sure of it now. Totally sure. "We did it!" I cried. I jumped up and down joyfully. "We killed the monster! We killed him!"

Clark reached into his back pocket — for his comic book, *Creatures from the Muck*. He hurled it across the room. It hit the monster in the head and fell to the floor.

"I never want to read about swamp monsters again. Never!" Clark cried. "Let's get out of here!"

Charley scratched at the door. When we opened it, he leaped out and jumped all over us. "It's okay, boy," I told him, trying to calm him down. "It's okay."

I peered into the room where we had locked Charley. "Hey, Clark, I think there's a door in here," I said. "A door that leads out!"

I stepped into the small, dark space — and stumbled over a broom lying on the floor.

I squinted in the darkness.

Two rusty shovels leaned against the wall to my right. On the left sat a coil of old hose.

In front of me I saw the door. A door with a large glass window.

I looked out the window — out to the backyard. To the path that ran through the swamp.

Does that path lead through the swamp to town? I wondered. I decided it was worth a try.

"We're almost out of here!" I declared. "We're almost free!"

I turned the doorknob, but the door was locked. Bolted from the other side, like all the doors in the house.

"It's jammed shut," I told Clark. "But I'll break the window and we'll climb out. No problem."

The shovels against the wall were big and heavy. I gripped the handle of one with both hands and took aim.

I swung it back — and felt the floor quake.

I spun around — and heard the roar.

The roar of the swamp monster.

He wasn't dead.

28

The creature rumbled into the doorway.

Clark and I both shrieked as he took a giant step into the room. His hideous head made a scraping sound as it brushed against the frame of the door. But he didn't even seem to notice.

Clark and I pressed against the wall.

Charley backed into a corner, whimpering. Frightened.

We were trapped.

No way out.

Nowhere to run.

The monster's eyes shifted from Charley, to me, to Clark. They rested on Clark for a moment. Then the creature lifted his head and wailed.

"He–he's going to get me first," Clark cried. "I — I shouldn't have thrown the comic at him. I shouldn't have hit him in the head."

"He's going to get *us*, you jerk!" I shouted at him. "Because *we* tried to *kill* him!"

That shut Clark up.

I have to do something, I thought. *I have to do something*. But what? *What?*

The swamp monster staggered forward.

He opened his snout with a snap — and bared jagged yellow teeth.

Sharp yellow teeth, dripping with saliva.

His eyes glowed red as he moved forward. Clomping closer and closer.

I glanced down and realized that I still held the shovel. I lifted it with two hands — and thrust it forward. Jabbing — jabbing at the air between the creature and me.

"Back!" I screamed. "Get back! Leave us alone!"

The monster grunted.

"Get back! Get back!" I swung the shovel wildly. "Go away!"

I swung at the creature.

I swung — and hit his stomach with a sickening *thwack*.

The room went silent.

Then the monster tossed back his head and let out a piercing howl.

He stumbled forward. Swiped the shovel from my hand. And tossed it out the door. Tossed it as if it were a toothpick.

I gasped as it crashed to the kitchen floor.

I eyed the other shovel leaning against the wall. The monster followed my gaze.

He snatched it up and broke it in half with his

bare hands. Then he pitched the pieces into the kitchen.

What can I do? I have to do something!

And then it came to me!

The letter.

The second letter from Grandma and Grandpa — the one we hadn't opened yet!

"Clark! Quick! The second letter," I cried. "Maybe it will tell us what to do! Read it!"

Clark stared at me. Frozen. His eyes on the raging monster.

"Clark!" I said, through clenched teeth. "Open . . . the . . . letter. NOW!"

He reached into his jeans pocket with a trembling hand. He fumbled with the flap.

"Hurry, Clark!" I pleaded.

He finally managed to tear a hole in the corner of the envelope.

And then I screamed.

The monster dove forward.

He grabbed my arm. He yanked it hard.

And pulled me toward him.

29

The monster pulled me close.

I stared up into his hideous face — and gasped.

His eyes were deep, dark pools — with tiny worms swimming in them!

I twisted my head away — so I wouldn't have to stare into those horrible, wormy eyes.

The creature gripped me tighter.

His hot, sour breath swept over my cheeks.

He opened his jaws wide.

His mouth was filled with bugs! I saw them crawling up and down his tongue.

I screamed. And struggled against the monster's hold. But he clutched me too tightly.

"Let me go!" I shrieked. "Please — !"

The monster bellowed in reply, hitting me with a blast of his hot breath.

He smells like a swamp, I realized as I fought against his grasp. *He is a swamp. He's like a living swamp.*

With my free hand, I pounded on the creature's arm. I nearly gagged when I felt the moss. His whole body was covered with a layer of wet moss!

"Let me go!" I pleaded. "Please — let me go!"

Clark leaped forward. He grabbed my arm and tried to tug me away. "Leave her alone!" he shrieked.

Charley charged out of his corner. His lip curled back and he let out a low snarl. Then he sank his teeth into the monster's hairy leg.

Startled, the monster jerked away, dragging me along with him.

But Charley wouldn't give up. I glanced down to see him dig his teeth deep into the monster's foot.

With a growl, the beast raised his foot. And with one fierce shake, he hurled Charley across the room.

"Charley!" I cried out. "Charley!"

I heard Charley whimper on the other side of the room.

"He's okay," Clark said, breathlessly. He tugged harder on my arm, trying to wrestle me free.

With another angry growl, the beast swung at Clark. Shoved him hard against the wall. Then the monster leaned down — and pulled me up to his face.

He opened his mouth.

His disgusting, bug-infested tongue rolled out. And he LICKED me.

He ran his hot, bumpy tongue up and down my arm.

Then he lowered his enormous teeth — as he prepared to chew off my hand.

30

"Nooooo!" A horrified shriek tore from my throat.

The monster's jaw swung down. His mouth gaped open. The bugs swarmed over his yellow teeth. He lowered his mouth to my hand.

Then he stopped.

And let me go.

He backed away, staring at me. Staring at my arm, eyes bulging.

I stared at my arm too. It was covered with disgusting, monster saliva.

The monster raised his hands and clutched at his throat now. Choking. Choking on something.

He raised his wet eyes to me.

"You — you human?" he choked out.

"He can *talk*!" Clark gasped.

"You human? You human?" he demanded.

"Y-yes, I'm a human," I stammered.

The monster threw back his head and groaned. "Oh, no. I'm *allergic* to humans."

His eyes rolled up.

He staggered forward and collapsed against the door to the outside. It crashed open under his heavy weight. Moonlight streamed in.

He lay there on his stomach. He didn't move.

I rubbed my wet arm and stared down at the swamp monster.

Was he really dead this time?

31

"Gretchen! Let's go!" Clark yanked me toward the open door.

We stepped over the monster. I glanced down at the creature one last time.

His eyes were shut. He didn't breathe. He didn't move.

"Come *on*, Gretchen!" Clark pleaded.

Is he really dead? I stared at the swamp monster. I wasn't totally sure. But I did know one thing — I wasn't going to hang around to find out.

Clark and I ran out through the broken door. We found Charley already there, waiting for us. We bolted down the path — away from the house. Into the swamp.

I was so surprised to find it was dark out. Had we really fought the swamp monster all day?

A pale moon hung over the cypress trees, casting an eerie glow over them.

The mud rose up over my ankles as we made

our way through the marshy ground. Through the tall weeds. Through a blanket of heavy mist.

My shoes plunged into deep pools of water. Tripped over upraised roots.

I swiped at the long beards of gray that hung from the trees. Swiped them from my face as we headed deeper and deeper into the swamp.

When the house was no longer in view, we stopped running. Stopped to catch our breath.

I listened in the darkness for footsteps.

The swamp monster's footsteps.

There weren't any.

"We did it! We killed the monster!" My voice rang out in the night.

"And we escaped!" Clark cheered. "We're free! We're okay!"

"Yes!" I shouted. "We really did it!"

Now that we had stopped running for our lives, we stepped through the swamp carefully. Leaping over the inky puddles and gnarled tree roots.

The night air echoed with strange sounds.

Low gurgling. Scampering footsteps. Piercing cries.

But I didn't care.

I had already battled my worst nightmare — the swamp monster. Battled him and won.

"Hey! Clark!" I suddenly remembered the other letter! "We never read Grandma and Grandpa's letter. The second letter!"

"So what?" Clark replied. "We don't have to

read it. The monster is dead. We killed it. Just as they told us to do in the first letter."

"Where is it? Where's the letter?" I demanded. "Take it out, Clark." I stopped walking. "I want to know what it says."

Clark pulled the crumpled envelope from his jeans pocket. As he smoothed out the wrinkles, a fierce animal cry cut through the swamp.

"I — I don't think we should stop now," Clark said. "We can read it later. After we reach town. After we call Mom and Dad."

"Read it now," I insisted. "Come on. Don't you want to know what it says?"

"No," Clark declared.

"Well, I do," I told him.

"Okay. Okay." Clark ripped open the envelope and slipped out the letter.

A light wind began to blow, carrying the sharp animal cries to us.

The dark trees rustled over our heads.

Clark began to read slowly, struggling to see in the dim moonlight. " 'Dear Gretchen and Clark. We hope you children are safe and well. We forgot one word of warning in the first letter.

" 'If the monster gets out . . . and you do kill it . . . and escape from the house — stay on the road. Do NOT go into the swamp.' "

Clark rolled his eyes. He let out a loud groan.

"Keep reading!" I shouted. "Read!"

He squinted in the dark and went on. " 'The

monster's brothers and sisters live in the swamp — dozens of them. We think they are out there. Waiting for him.' "

My heart started to race as Clark continued.

" 'We've seen the monsters in the swamp. We've heard them whistling to each other every night. They're unhappy their brother was captured. They're waiting for him to return. So whatever you do, stay out of the swamp. It's not safe out there. Stay out of the swamp! Good luck! We love you.' "

Clark's hands dropped to his sides. The letter fell to the marshy ground.

I turned slowly, staring out at the shifting shadows.

"Gretchen." Clark choked out my name. "Do you hear that? What is that sound? What is it?"

"Uh . . . it sounds like a whistle."

"Th-that's what I thought," he whispered. "What do we do now? Any ideas?"

"No, Clark," I replied softly. "I don't have any more ideas. How about you?"

Add *more*

Goosebumps®

to your collection . . .

Here's a chilling preview of

THE BARKING GHOST

2

I didn't move.

I *couldn't* move.

I stared at the ceiling. Listening. Listening to the raspy breathing under my bed.

Okay, Cooper, I told myself. Calm down. It's probably your imagination. Playing tricks on you again.

The breathing grew louder. Raspier.

I covered my ears and shut my eyes tight.

It's nothing. It's nothing. It's nothing.

It's an old house, I thought, still covering my ears. Old houses have to breathe — don't they?

Or, what was it that Mom said? Settling? Yeah, that's what it must be. The house settling.

Or maybe it's the pipes. We had pipes in our apartment in Boston, and they made crazy noises all the time. I'll bet that's what it is — the pipes.

I lowered my hands.

Silence now. No settling. No pipes. No breathing.

I must be losing my mind.

If I told Gary and Todd about this one, they'd really laugh their heads off.

And then the breathing started again. Raspy and wet. Hoarse breathing. Like a sick animal.

I couldn't just lie there. I had to see what it was.

I swung my legs out of bed. I took a deep breath. Then I lowered myself to the floor.

Carefully, I lifted the blanket from the bottom of the bed. Then carefully, carefully, I lowered my head and peeked under the bed.

That's when the hands darted out — and grabbed me. Two strong, cold hands. Slowly tightening their grip around my throat.

3

I screamed.

So loudly, I surprised myself.

My attacker must have been surprised, too. He quickly let go of my neck. I clutched my throat and sputtered for air.

"Cooper, will you keep it down?" a voice whispered. "You'll wake Mom and Dad!"

Huh?

Oh, man.

It was Mickey. My totally obnoxious older brother.

"Mickey! You jerk!" I cried. "You scared me to death!"

Mickey slid out from under the bed and wiped some dust off his pajamas. "No big challenge," he muttered.

"Shut up," I snapped, rubbing my sore neck. In the mirror I could see where Mickey's hands had grabbed my throat. Dark red blotches circled my neck.

"Look what you did!" I cried. "You *know* I bruise easily!"

"Oh, don't be such a baby! I got you, man!" Mickey cried, grinning.

I stared furiously at my idiot brother. I wished I could wipe that grin off his face. And not get in trouble for it.

"You're a jerk!" was all I could think to say.

"Grow up!" Mickey shot back. He headed for the door, then turned around. "Would Cooper like a little night-light next to his bed?" he asked in a tiny baby voice.

That's when I lost it.

I leaped on to his back and pounded his head with my fists.

"Hey!" he screamed, trying to shake me off. "What do you think you're doing? Get off me!"

Mickey's legs buckled under him, and he fell to the floor. I clung to his back. I kept pounding him with my fists.

Mickey is three years older than me, and he's a lot bigger. But I had him in the right position, and landed a few good punches.

Then he shifted to the right.

And started pounding me back. Luckily, he got

in only one really good wallop before Mom and Dad ran in to break it up.

"Cooper! Mickey! What's going on in here?"

"He started it!" I called out, trying to duck Mickey's fists.

My father reached down and pulled Mickey off me. "I don't care who started it!" he said angrily. "This is no way to act on the first night in your new house. Mickey, get back to your room!"

"But, Dad, he —"

"Never mind who started it. This behavior had better stop — now! Because if there is a *next* time, you'll both start off the new school year grounded!"

Grumbling, Mickey stomped out of the room. But not before sticking his tongue out at me. Mickey was the baby. Not me.

"Really, Dad, Mickey started it," I said when he was gone.

"And you're totally innocent, right?" my father asked, rolling his eyes.

"Yes!" I insisted.

Dad just shook his head. "Go to sleep, Cooper."

When my parents left the room, I paced back and forth, rubbing my neck.

I was so steamed!

It wasn't the first time Mickey's pulled something like this. For as long as I can remember, Mickey has played tricks on me, trying to terrify me.

He usually succeeds, too.

Once, when Mom and Dad went away for a weekend, he hid a tape recorder in my room. It played horrifying screams all night long.

And another time, he didn't come to get me after Little League practice. He left me standing there, all alone on the playground, while he hid out and watched me panic.

But hiding under my bed tonight was the worst. He has to be one of the biggest jerks alive.

I climbed back into bed and stared up at the ceiling. I had to think of a way to get Mickey back.

What could I do? Hide outside his window and scream?

Jump out from behind the shower curtain when he's brushing his teeth?

No. Too dumb. It would have to be something totally excellent. Something so creepy it would scare me. Even though I was the one doing it.

I watched the spooky shadows move along my walls and ceiling. And listened to the frightening noises of my new house — noises I would have to hear for the rest of my life.

The pipes rattling. The dogs barking.

Wait a minute.

Dogs?

I sat up. We don't have a dog. And there isn't another house around here for miles.

But I definitely heard a barking dog.

I listened closely. The dog barked again. Then started to howl.

I sighed and pulled off the covers again. I started to climb out of bed. Then it hit me.

Mickey!

This had to be another one of my brother's stupid tricks. He was an excellent dog-barker. He practiced it all the time.

Smiling, I settled back on my pillow. I wouldn't get up. I wouldn't go to the window.

He wasn't going to get me this time. No way.

I lay there listening to Mickey make a fool of himself. Howling and barking like a big old dog.

What a jerk.

Then, suddenly, I sat up again. Whoa. I heard *two* dogs howling now.

Even Mickey couldn't pull that off.

The howling turned to piercing cries. So close. Right under my window.

As I said, I made it through a whole day without being scared. But, boy, was I making up for it tonight!

For the zillionth and third time, I slowly crept

to the window. I could hear them clearly. Two dogs. Wailing and howling.

For the zillionth and third time, I gazed out the window.

But for the *first* time, I couldn't believe what I saw.

4

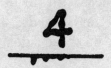

I didn't see anything.

Nothing at all. No dogs. Not one.

I squinted into the yard. Empty.

How could they have vanished so quickly?

I stood at the window for a few more seconds, but no dogs appeared.

I shivered. I'll never sleep again, I thought. Not as long as I have to live here.

I crept back to bed. I pulled the covers up to my chin. And counted the green and blue squigglies on the wallpaper by my head.

I guess I finally fell asleep. When I opened my eyes, light streamed in through my window.

Yawning, I glanced at the clock. Six-thirty. I'm usually an early bird. I like to start my day as soon as possible.

I leaped out of bed and checked the yard. It didn't seem half as scary in the morning light.

I smiled when I noticed the jungle gym in the

far corner. The last owners of the house built it. It had a slide and really high monkey bars. Yesterday, Dad hung a rope and tire from one of its beams, so now it had a swing, too.

Behind the jungle gym, the woods stretched all around. Woods thick with all different kinds of trees and shrubs and weeds. The woods surrounded our house on three sides. It seemed to go on forever.

I changed quickly, pulling a clean Red Sox T-shirt over my jeans. Grabbing my baseball cap, I flew through the house and ran outside.

A great summer day! Sunny and warm. If I were back home in Boston, I would hop on my bike and ride over to Gary's or Todd's house. Then we would spend the day outdoors, playing softball at the playground. Or just messing around.

But I'm not in Boston anymore. Better get used to that, I told myself.

I hoped some cool kids lived in this neighborhood. When we drove up to our house yesterday, I didn't see any other houses around. I guessed I'd have to spend the next few days alone — until school started next week.

I wandered over to the jungle gym. I swung on the tire swing for a little while. Back and forth. Back and forth. Staring at my bedroom window from the outside. Back and forth. Back and forth. Remembering last night.

Remembering just how brave Super Cooper had been. Yuck!

Back and forth. Back and forth.

Remembering the dogs.

Hey. That's weird, I thought. Those dogs I heard should have left paw prints all over the yard. But I couldn't see a single one.

I hopped off the swing and searched the ground all around the house. No sign of any dogs.

That's funny. I *knew* there were dogs out here last night.

I glanced up at the edge of the woods. Maybe those dogs were lost, I thought. Maybe they came to the house last night searching for help.

Maybe I should go track them down.

I bit my lower lip. A kid could lose his way — forever — in those woods. I thought nervously.

Well, I'm going in, I decided. Today is the first day of the new me. Super Cooper — for real. I wanted to find those dogs. To prove to myself that I wasn't going crazy.

Who knows? If I find the dogs, maybe Dad will let me keep one, I decided. It might be fun to have a dog.

I'd always wanted a puppy. But Mom said the fur made her sneeze. Maybe she'd change her mind.

I took one long, deep breath. Then I stepped into the woods. I saw some amazing trees. I saw beautiful old birch trees with smooth, white trunks. And I saw sassafras and maple trees. Their trunks were gnarled and thick.

They could be over a hundred years old, I thought. Awesome.

Maybe Dad can build a tree house back here, I told myself excitedly. That would be so cool. Then when Gary and Todd came to visit, we could hang out in it.

I kept my eyes on the ground as I walked searching for any sign of dogs.

Nothing. No prints. No broken branches.

How weird. I definitely heard dogs last night.

Or maybe I just *thought* I'd heard those dogs. It *was* kind of late, and I *was* pretty sleepy. Maybe it was my imagination.

Or maybe it was Mickey after all.

Maybe he tape-recorded another dog and barked along with it.

He would do something like that.

He's that sneaky.

I really had to pay him back. Something way creepy. Maybe I could do something out here in the woods.

I made my way through the thick trees and tall weeds, the whole time thinking of how to scare Mickey.

I suddenly realized I hadn't been paying attention to where I was going.

I spun around and peered through the thick trunks.

My house! I couldn't see it!

Okay, Cooper, keep cool. You can't be that far away, I told myself.

But my palms began to sweat.

I swallowed hard, then tried to remember which way I'd come.

Definitely the left.

No, wait. Maybe right.

I hung my head and moaned. It's no use, I thought.

I'm lost. Hopelessly lost.

5

I really didn't want to cry.

Who needed Mickey seeing me with wet, red eyes?

I'd never heard the end of it.

Besides, today was the first day of the new me. The new Super Cooper.

I took a really deep breath and tried to calm down.

I decided to walk a little to my right. If I didn't see my house, I'd turn and double back to the left.

It was worth a try.

What did I have to lose? I was lost anyway.

I turned to the right. I tried to take the straightest path possible.

The snapping of branches behind me made me spin around.

No one there.

It's just a harmless squirrel or something, I told myself. Just keep going.

I returned to my straight path again. But with my first step, I heard leaves rustling behind me.

I didn't turn around. I quickened my pace.

And I heard it again.

Twigs snapping. Leaves rustling.

My throat suddenly felt dry. Don't panic. Don't panic. "Wh-who's there?" I croaked.

No answer.

I turned back.

Whoa! Which way had I been walking? My head began to spin. I suddenly felt dizzy. Too dizzy to remember where I had been.

Snap. Snap. Crack. Crunch.

"Who is there?" I called out again. My voice didn't sound all that steady for Super Cooper.

"Mickey, is that you? This isn't funny! Mickey?"

Then I felt something horrible scrape my cheek. Something cold. And sharp.

I couldn't help it. I started to scream.

6

A leaf. A dumb leaf.

Come on, Cooper! Get a grip!

I sat down on the ground for a second. I checked my watch. It was almost eight.

Dad would be out in the yard soon. He planned to set up the new barbecue grill first thing this morning. I figured I could just wait for the hammering to start, then walk in the direction of the noise.

I'd just sit here. And wait. Wait for the hammering. Good idea, I thought.

I heard something rustle behind me.

Just the leaves, I told myself. The dumb leaves.

I stole a glance up at the trees. I tilted my head way back — and someone grabbed my arm.

I jerked away. Sprang up. Started to run.

And tripped over my own feet.

Scrambling up, I gasped in surprise.

A girl.

She was about my age and had really long, red hair. It was frizzy, and it stuck out in a million directions. She had big green eyes. She wore a bright red T-shirt and red shorts. She reminded me of a rag doll Todd's little sister used to carry around.

"You okay?" she asked, her hands on her waist.

"Yeah, sure. Fine," I muttered.

"Didn't mean to scare you," she said.

"I wasn't scared," I lied.

"Really," she said. "I would have been scared, too, if someone grabbed me like that. I really didn't mean to."

"I told you," I said sharply, "I wasn't scared."

"Okay. Sorry."

"What are you sorry about?" I asked. This had to be the weirdest girl I'd ever met.

"I don't know," she replied, shrugging. "I'm just sorry."

"Well, you can stop apologizing," I told her. I brushed the dirt off my clothes and picked up my baseball cap. I quickly set it back on my head. To cover my ears.

The girl stared at me. She stood there and stared. Without saying a word. Was she staring at my ears?

"Who are you?" I finally asked.

"Margaret Ferguson," she replied. "But people call me Fergie. Like the duchess."

I didn't know what duchess she was talking about. But I pretended I did.

"I live through the woods that way," she said, pointing behind her.

"I thought no one lived around here for miles," I said.

"Yeah. There are some houses around here, Cooper," she replied. "They're pretty spread out."

"Hey! How did you know my name?" I asked suspiciously.

Margaret, or Fergie, or whatever her name was, turned beet-red.

"I, uh, watched you move in yesterday," she confessed.

"I didn't see you," I replied.

"That's because I hid in the woods," she said. "I heard your father call you Cooper. And I know your last name, too. It's Holmes. I saw it written on all the boxes in the moving van. And I know you have a brother, Mickey," she added. "He's a jerk."

I laughed. "You got that right!" I exclaimed. "So how long have you lived around here?"

She didn't answer. She kept her eyes on the ground.

"I said, how long have —"

Suddenly, her head jerked up and she gazed into my eyes.

"Wh-what's wrong?" I asked when I saw her frightened face.

Her face tightened, as if she were in pain. Her lips trembled.

"Margaret!" I cried. "What? What is it?"

She opened her mouth, but no words came out. She breathed deeply, gulping air. Finally, she clutched my shoulders and shoved her face right up close to mine.

"Dogs," she whispered. Then she let go of me and darted away.

I froze for a moment. Then I chased after her.

She made it to a big tree stump before I caught up. I grabbed hold of the back of her T-shirt and spun her around.

"Margaret, what do you mean 'dogs'?" I asked.

"No! No!" she cried. "Just let me go! Let me go!"

I held her tightly.

"Let me go! Let me go!" she cried again.

"Margaret, what did you mean back there?" I repeated. "This is important. Why did you say 'dogs'?"

"Dogs?" Her eyes grew wide. "I don't remember saying that."

My jaw fell open. "You did!" I insisted. "You looked straight at me and said, 'dogs'! I heard you!"

She shook her head. "No, I don't remember that," she replied thoughtfully.

Now I've met weird kids in my life, but Margaret here takes the cake. She almost makes Mickey seem normal.

Almost.

"Okay," I said, trying to sound calm, "here's what happened. You freaked out. Then you grabbed me. Then you said, 'Dogs.' Then you freaked out again."

"Don't remember," she replied softly, shaking her head from side to side. "Why would I say that?"

"I don't know!" I screamed, starting to lose it. "I'm not the one who said it!"

She gazed around in all directions, then focused those green, crazy eyes on me.

"Listen to me, Cooper," she whispered mysteriously. "Get away from here."

"Huh?"

"I'm warning you, Cooper. Tell your parents they must leave at once!" She glanced nervously behind her, then turned back to me.

"Please — listen to me. Get away from here! As fast as you can!"

About the Author

R.L. STINE is the author of the series *Fear Street, Nightmare Room, Give Yourself Goosebumps,* and the phenomenally successful *Goosebumps.* His thrilling teen titles have sold more than 250 million copies internationally — enough to earn him a spot in the *Guinness Book of World Records*! Mr. Stine lives in New York City with his wife, Jane, and his son, Matt.

Collect Them All!
Goosebumps®
By R.L. Stine

- ❑ Goosebumps: Abominable Snowman of Pasadena
- ❑ Goosebumps: Attack of the Jack-O-Lanterns
- ❑ Goosebumps: Attack of The Mutant
- ❑ Goosebumps: Bad Hare Day
- ❑ Goosebumps: Barking Ghost
- ❑ Goosebumps: The Beast from the East
- ❑ Goosebumps: Be Careful What You Wish For...
- ❑ Goosebumps: The Cuckoo Clock of Doom
- ❑ Goosebumps: The Curse of Camp Cold Lake
- ❑ Goosebumps: Curse of the Mummy's Tomb
- ❑ Goosebumps: Deep Trouble
- ❑ Goosebumps: Egg Monsters from Mars
- ❑ Goosebumps: Ghost Beach
- ❑ Goosebumps: Ghost Camp
- ❑ Goosebumps: Ghost Next Door
- ❑ Goosebumps: The Girl Who Cried Monster
- ❑ Goosebumps: Go Eat Worms!
- ❑ Goosebumps: The Haunted Mask
- ❑ Goosebumps: The Haunted Mask II
- ❑ Goosebumps: The Headless Ghost
- ❑ Goosebumps: The Horror at Camp Jellyjam
- ❑ Goosebumps: How I Got My Shrunken Head
- ❑ Goosebumps: How to Kill a Monster
- ❑ Goosebumps: It Came from Beneath the Sink!
- ❑ Goosebumps: Lets Get Invisible
- ❑ Goosebumps: Monster Blood
- ❑ Goosebumps: Monster Blood II
- ❑ Goosebumps: A Night in Terror Tower
- ❑ Goosebumps: Night of the Living Dummy
- ❑ Goosebumps: Night of the Living Dummy II
- ❑ Goosebumps: Night of the Living Dummy III
- ❑ Goosebumps: One Day at HorrorLand
- ❑ Goosebumps: Piano Lessons Can Be Murder
- ❑ Goosebumps: Revenge of the Lawn Gnomes
- ❑ Goosebumps: Say Cheese and Die!
- ❑ Goosebumps: Say Cheese and Die — Again!
- ❑ Goosebumps: The Scarecrow Walks at Midnight
- ❑ Goosebumps: Shocker on Shock Street
- ❑ Goosebumps: Stay Out of the Basement
- ❑ Goosebumps: Vampire Breath
- ❑ Goosebumps: Welcome to Camp Nightmare
- ❑ Goosebumps: Welcome to Dead House
- ❑ Goosebumps: The Werewolf of Fever Swamp
- ❑ Goosebumps: Why I'm Afraid of Bees
- ❑ Goosebumps: You Can't Scare Me!

▦ SCHOLASTIC

GBKLST0805

Read at Your Own Risk

Goosebumps

By R. L. Stine

____ 0-439-72705-8 **Goosebumps: Attack of the Jack-O-Lanterns**

____ 0-439-66215-X **Goosebumps: Attack of The Mutant**

____ 0-439-66216-8 **Goosebumps: Bad Hare Day**

____ 0-439-66990-1 **Goosebumps: Be Careful What You Wish For**

____ 0-439-72403-1 **Goosebumps: The Beast from the East**

____ 0-439-72404-X **Goosebumps: The Curse of Camp Cold Lake**

____ 0-439-56828-5 **Goosebumps: Deep Trouble**

____ 0-439-56829-3 **Goosebumps: Egg Monsters from Mars**

____ 0-439-56830-7 **Goosebumps: Ghost Beach**

____ 0-439-56831-5 **Goosebumps: Ghost Camp**

____ 0-439-69353-5 **Goosebumps: The Girl Who Cried Monster**

____ 0-439-67114-0 **Goosebumps: Go Eat Worms!**

____ 0-439-67113-2 **Goosebumps: The Haunted Mask II**

____ 0-439-66987-1 **Goosebumps: The Headless Ghost**

____ 0-439-56837-4 **Goosebumps: It Came from Beneath the Sink!**

____ 0-439-66988-X **Goosebumps: Monster Blood II**

____ 0-439-67111-6 **Goosebumps: A Night in Terror Tower**

____ 0-439-57374-2 **Goosebumps: Night of the Living Dummy II**

____ 0-439-66989-8 **Goosebumps: Night of the Living Dummy III**

____ 0-439-56841-2 **Goosebumps: One Day at HorrorLand**

____ 0-439-67112-4 **Goosebumps: Piano Lessons Can Be Murder**

____ 0-439-57375-0 **Goosebumps: Revenge of the Lawn Gnomes**

____ 0-439-56842-0 **Goosebumps: Say Cheese and Die!**

____ 0-439-57361-0 **Goosebumps: Say Cheese and Die—Again!**

____ 0-439-56843-9 **Goosebumps: The Scarecrow Walks at Midnight**

____ 0-439-72706-6 **Goosebumps: Vampire Breath**

____ 0-439-56846-3 **Goosebumps: Welcome to Camp Nightmare**

____ 0-439-56848-X **Goosebumps: The Werewolf of Fever Swamp**

____ 0-439-57365-3 **Goosebumps: You Can't Scare Me!**

____ 0-439-69354-3 **Goosebumps: Why Im Afraid of Bees**

Available Wherever Books Are Sold, or Use This Order Form.

▲ SCHOLASTIC